Cosmic Storm

Tor Teen Books by Dom Testa

GALAHAD

The Comet's Curse
The Web of Titan
The Cassini Code
The Dark Zone
Cosmic Storm
The Galahad Legacy (forthcoming)

A GALAHAD BOOK

Cosmic
Storm

Dom Testa

TOR®
TEEN

A Tom Doherty Associates Book
New York

COSMIC STORM

Copyright © 2011 by Dom Testa

The Galahad Legacy excerpt copyright © 2011 by Dom Testa

Reader's Guide copyright © 2011 by Tor Books

A Tor® Teen Book
Published by Tom Doherty Associates, LLC
175 Fifth Avenue
New York, NY 10010

www.tor-forge.com

Tor® is a registered trademark of Tom Doherty Associates, LLC.

ISBN 978-0-7653-2111-4

First Edition: October 2011

Printed in the United States of America

0 9 8 7 6 5 4 3 2 1

For Monica

Acknowledgments

As always, thanks to the cool folks at Tor who are taking this voyage with me: Kathleen Doherty, Tom Doherty, Susan Chang, and countless others behind the scenes.

I owe a debt of gratitude to Judith Briles and Jacques de Spoelbergh for getting Galahad out of Colorado and onto the big stage.

Also thanks to the many schools around the country who have climbed aboard the Galahad mission, and taken the adventure— and their students—to a new level.

I'm especially grateful to my son, Dominic III, for his continuous help, his visionary ideas and writing, and his diligence in making this book series accessible to so many. No father could be more proud.

And last, but certainly not least, thanks to everyone, both young and old, who believe in the books and their message. Smart is indeed cool. Spread the word.

Cosmic
Storm

The universe doesn't play fair. It supposedly has all of these rules which we're expected to obediently follow, and yet when you turn your head the universe sneaks in a few new rules that completely contradict the first set. It's like playing a game with a four-year-old.

For instance, the universe has one set of rules for very big things, like stars and planets and galaxies and government waste, and then another set of rules for very little things, like subatomic particles and boy-band talent.

But don't get too comfortable with either set, because the universe reserves the right to mix them up and make exceptions whenever it feels like it, and it doesn't even have to tell you. Take wormholes, for instance . . .

Actually, before we get to the wormholes, let's cover some basic territory. There's a chance you have randomly picked up this particular volume and you're wondering what you've stumbled into. Don't feel bad, those of us on the ship often have that same feeling.

The ship, by the way, is called Galahad, and it's only the most spectacular spacecraft ever built by human hands. *To truly understand the story of what it is, and where it's going, and who's on board, you should probably stop now, go dig up the first volume—titled* The Comet's Curse—*and start from the beginning. That's followed by* The Web of Titan, The Cassini Code, *and* The Dark Zone. *They're each a rollicking, riveting tale of mystery and adventure, if I do say so myself.*

If you're stubborn and insist on diving in right here, let me do my best to catch you up.

Deadly particles in the tail of the comet Bhaktul contaminated Earth's atmosphere, delivering a death sentence that threatened to wipe out the human species. But when it was determined that kids were immune until about the age of eighteen, a plan was hatched to select a few hundred of the world's best and brightest teenagers and launch them towards the star system known as Eos, where two Earthlike planets would await them. Galahad *became their lifeboat to the stars.*

Our brave pioneers had barely pulled out of the cosmic driveway when trouble raised its head in the form of a sinister stowaway, someone determined to destroy the ship. Oh, but wait; after that crisis, more trouble popped up during their rendezvous with a research station near Saturn. It was here that the crew of Galahad *encountered an alien lifeform known as the Cassini, beings of almost pure thought that could either help the teens, or destroy them.*

Following that little conflict came a terrifying trip through a minefield of debris in the outer ring of the solar system known as the Kuiper Belt. It was during this death-defying dash through the boulder-strewn obstacle course that tempers flared and sides were drawn. Some crew members wanted to turn back, some opted to press onward. Let's just say it got very, very ugly.

When we last left our merry star travelers, they had just confronted another alien species, a creepy collection of creatures that were labeled "vultures," and were responsible for Galahad's first death. The vultures came and went through some of the most bizarre features in the universe: wormholes. These act like cosmic secret passageways and have a nasty habit of opening and closing when you least expect them to. In fact, the ship's Council Leader, Triana Martell, just recently disappeared through a wormhole which immediately folded up and vanished.

The remaining Council members—Gap Lee, Lita Marques, Channy Oakland, and Bon Hartsfield—must now carry on without their vaunted leader, who may—or may not—return. Their relationships are about to get tested to the max. Plus, don't be surprised if some old friends from earlier adventures resurface.

I'll be along for the ride, too. My name is Roc, and I wear a variety of hats on the ship. Yes, I'm the computer brain that is responsible for the lights and the heat and the gravity and lots of other boring, mundane tasks. But I happen to believe that my greatest duty—my calling, if you will—is in the role of advisor, therapist, confidant, and aquatics instructor.

That puts me in the front row for the greatest adventure of all time. You're invited to join us, too. Just find a way to balance on the edge of a seat, and remember our little talk about wormholes and rules. I think you'll discover that rules change for people, too, depending upon what suits them at the time.

I might be a complex machine, but you humans are just plain complicated.

I t was actual paper, something that was a rarity on the ship. It measured, in inches, approximately six by nine, but had been folded twice into a compact rectangle. One word—the name Gap—was scrawled along the outside of the paper, in a distinctive style that could have come from only one person aboard *Galahad*. The loop on the final letter was not entirely closed, which made it more than an *r* but just short of a *p*; a casual reader would assume that the writer was in a hurry.

Gap Lee knew that it was simply the way Triana Martell wrote. It wasn't so much impatience on her part, but a conservation of energy. Her version of the letter *b* suffered the same fate, giving the impression of an extended *h*. It took some getting used to, but eventually Gap was able to read the scribbles without stumbling too much.

And, because he had scoured this particular note at least twenty times, it was now practically memorized anyway.

He looked at it again, this time under the tight beam of the desk lamp. It was just after midnight, and the rest of the room was dark. His roommate, Daniil, lay motionless in his bed across the room, a very faint snore seeping out from beneath the pillow that covered his head. With a full crew meeting only eight hours away, and having chalked up perhaps a total of six hours of sleep over the past two days, Gap knew that he should be tucked into his own bed. Yet while his eyelids felt heavy, his brain would not shut down.

He exhaled a long, slow breath. How just like Triana to forego sending an e-mail and instead scratch out her explanation to Gap by hand. She journaled, like many of the crew members on *Galahad*, but was the only one who did so the old-fashioned way, in a notebook rather than on her workpad. This particular note had been ripped from the binding of a notebook, its rough edges adding a touch that Gap could only describe as personal.

He found that he appreciated the intimate feel, while he detested the message itself. The opening line alone was enough to cause him angst.

> Gap, I know that my decision will likely anger you and the other Council members, but in my opinion there was no time for debate, especially one that would more than likely end in a stalemate.

Of course he was angry. Triana had made one of her "executive decisions" again, a snap judgment that might have proved fatal. The rest of the ship's ruling body, the Council, had expressed a variety of emotions, ranging from disbelief to despair; if they were angry, it wasn't bubbling to the surface yet.

Now, sitting in the dark and staring at the note, Gap pushed aside his personal feelings—feelings that were mostly confused anyway—and tried to focus on the upcoming meeting. More than two hundred crew members were going to be on edge, alarmed that the ship's Council Leader had plunged into a wormhole, nervous that there was little to no information about whether she could even survive the experience. They were desperate for direction; it would be his job to calm them, assure them, and deliver answers.

It was simply a matter of coming up with those answers in the next few hours.

He stood and stretched, casting a quick glance at Daniil, who mumbled something in his sleep and turned to face the wall. Gap leaned over his desk and moved Triana's note into the small circle of light. His eyes darted through the message one more time, then folded it back into its original shape. He snapped off the light and stumbled to his bed. Draping one arm over his eyes, he tried to block everything from his mind and settle into a relaxed state. Sleep was the most important thing at the moment, and he was sure that he was the only Council member still awake at this time of the night.

He wasn't. Lita Marques had every intention of being asleep by ten, and had planned on an early morning workout in the gym before breakfast and the crew meeting. But now it was past midnight, and she found herself walking into *Galahad*'s clinic, usually referred to by the crew as Sick House. It was under her supervision, a role that came naturally to the daughter of a physician.

Walking in the door she was greeted with surprise by Mathias, an assistant who tonight manned the late shift.

"What are you doing here?" he said, quickly dragging his feet off his desk and sitting upright.

"No, please, put your feet back up," Lita said with a smile. "You know we're very informal here, especially in the dead of night." She walked over to her own desk and plopped down. "And to answer your question . . . I don't know. Couldn't sleep, so I decided to maybe work for a bit."

Mathias squinted at her. "You doing okay with everything? I mean . . . with Alexa . . . and Tree. I mean . . ."

"Yeah, I'm fine. Thanks for asking, though." She moved a couple of things around on her desk. "It's just . . . you know, we'll get through it all just fine."

A moment of awkward silence fell between them. Lita continued to shuffle things in front of her, then realized how foolish it looked. She chanced a quick glance towards Mathias and caught his concerned look. "Really," she said.

And then she broke down. Seeming to come from nowhere, a sob burst from her, and she covered her face with her hands. A minute later she felt a presence, and lowered her hands to find Mathias kneeling beside her.

"I'm so sorry," he said quietly. "What can I do?"

"There's nothing you can do. But thank you." Suddenly embarrassed, she funneled all of her energy into looking composed and under control. "Really, it's probably just a lack of sleep, and . . . well, you know."

Mathias shook his head. "I don't want to speak out of place, but you don't have to act tough in front of me. We're talking about losing your two best friends within a matter of days. There's no doubt that you need some sleep, but it's more than that. And that's okay, Lita."

She nodded and put a worried smile on her face. "You know what? Sometimes I wish I wasn't on the Council; I think sometimes we're too concerned with being a good example, and we forget to be ourselves."

"Well, you can always be yourself around me," he said, moving from her side and dropping into the chair facing her desk. He picked up a glass cube on her desk, the one filled with sand and tiny pebbles taken from the beach near Lita's home in Veracruz, Mexico. She found that not only did it bring her comfort, it attracted almost everyone who sat at her desk.

Mathias twisted the cube to one side, watching the sand tumble, forming multicolored layers of sediment. "So, I'll be curious to see what Gap says at this meeting," he said, never taking his eyes off the cube. He left the comment floating between them.

"I don't envy Gap right now," Lita said cautiously. "We've been through so much in this first year, but especially in the last two weeks." She paused and stared at her assistant. "I know everyone's curious about what he intends to do, but there's not much I can say right now."

Mathias shrugged and placed the glass cube back on her desk. "I guess a few of us just wondered if he was going to become the new Council Leader."

"He's temporarily in charge. But we don't know for sure what's happened to Triana. She's still the Council Leader."

"Well, yeah, of course," Mathias said. "But . . ." He looked up at her. "I mean, she disappeared into a wormhole. Could she even survive that?"

Lita's first instinct was irritation; Triana had been gone for forty-eight hours, and Mathias seemed to have written her off. And, if so, chances were that he wasn't alone. It was likely, in fact, that when the auditorium filled up in the morning, many of the crew members would be under the assumption that *Galahad*'s leader was dead. It would have been unthinkable only days ago, but . . .

But they had stood in silence to pay their final respects to Alexa just hours before Triana's flight. Now anything seemed possible.

The realization cooled Lita's temper. It wasn't Mathias's fault; he was merely acting upon a natural human emotion. Lita's defense of Triana stemmed from an entirely different, but no less powerful, emotion: loyalty to a friend.

When she finally spoke, her voice was soft. "This crew has learned pretty quickly that when we jump to conclusions, we're usually wrong. I'm sure Gap will do a good job of explaining things so we know what's going on and what we can look forward to. Let's just wait until the meeting before we assume too much."

Mathias gave a halfhearted nod. "Yeah. Okay." Slowly, a sheepish look crossed his face. "And I'm sorry. Triana's your friend; I shouldn't be saying this stuff. I'm just . . ."

"It's all right," Lita said. "We're all shaken up. Now let me do a little work so I can wear myself out enough to sleep."

Once the clock in her room clicked over to midnight, Channy Oakland climbed out of bed, threw on a pair of shorts and a vivid red T-shirt, woke up the cat, Iris, who was contorted into a ball on her desk chair, and trudged to the lift at the end of the hall. Two minutes later, carrying Iris over her shoulder like a baby, she peered through the murky light of Dome 1. There was no movement.

Two massive domes topped the starship, housing the Farms and providing a daily bounty which fed the hungry crew of teenagers. Clear panels, set among a criss-crossing grid of beams, allowed a spectacular view of the cosmos to shine in and quickly became a favorite spot for crew quiet time.

It was especially quiet at this late hour. Channy could see a couple of farm workers milling about in the distance, but for the most part Dome 1 was deserted. She took her usual route down a well-trodden path, and deposited Iris near a dense patch of corn stalks. "See you in twenty minutes," she said in a hushed tone to the cat, then, on a whim, retreated towards the main entrance. She turned off the path and made for the Farms' offices.

Her instinct had been right on. Lights burned in Bon's office. She leaned against the door frame and glanced at the tall boy who stood behind the desk. "Something told me I'd find you here," she said.

Bon Hartsfield glanced up only briefly before turning back to a glowing workpad. "Not unusual for me to be here, day or night," he said. "You know that. The question is, what are you doing up here this late. Wait, let me guess: cat duty."

"Couldn't sleep. Figured I might as well let Iris stretch her legs."

Bon grunted a reply, but seemed bored by the exchange. Channy took a couple of steps into the office, her hands in her back pockets. "How are you doing?"

He looked up at her, but this time his gaze lingered. "Wanna be more specific?"

She shrugged, then took two more steps towards his desk. "Oh, you know; Alexa, Triana . . . everything."

He looked back down at his workpad. His shaggy blond hair draped over his face. "I'm doing fine. Sorry, but I have to check out a water recycling pump." He walked around his desk towards the door.

"Mind if I walk along with you?" Channy said. "I have to pick up Iris in a few minutes anyway."

"Suit yourself," he said without stopping.

His strides were long and quick. She hustled to keep up until he veered from the path into a thick growth of leafy plants. It was even darker here; she was happy when Bon flicked on a flashlight, its tightly focused beam bobbing back and forth before them. The air was warm and damp, and the heavy vegetation around them blocked much of the ventilating breeze. Channy felt sweat droplets on her chocolate-toned skin.

"You would have loved Lita's song—"

"Why are you whispering?" he called back to her.

"I don't know, it's very quiet and peaceful in here. All right, I'll speak up. I said that you would have loved Lita's song for Alexa at the funeral." When he didn't respond, but instead continued to push ahead through the gloom, she added, "But I understand why you weren't there."

"I'm so glad. It would have wrecked my day if you were upset with me."

"Okay, Mr. Sarcastic. I'm just trying to talk to you."

"Next subject."

A leafy branch slapped back against Channy's face. "Ouch. Excuse me, is this a race?"

"You wanted to come, I didn't invite you."

They popped out of the heavy growth into a diamond-shaped clearing. Bon stopped quickly, and Channy barely managed to throw on the brakes without plowing into his back. A moment later he was down on one knee. "Here," he said, holding the flashlight out to her. "If you want to tag along, do something helpful. Point this right here."

She trained the light on the two-foot-tall block that housed a water recycling pump. One of the precious resources on *Galahad*, water was closely monitored and conserved. Every drop was recycled, which meant these particular pumps were crucial under the domes. After a handful of breakdowns early in the mission, they were now checked constantly.

"I guess Gap will try to explain at the meeting what Tree did," Channy said, sitting down on the loosely packed soil. She kept the flashlight trained on the pump, but occasionally shifted her grasp in order to throw a bit of light towards Bon's face. "Although I have to admit, I don't think I'll ever understand why she did it."

She waited for Bon to respond, but he seemed to want nothing to do with the conversation. She added, "Do you think she did the right thing?"

"Keep the light steady right here," he said. For half a minute he toiled in silence before finally answering her. "It doesn't matter what I think. Triana did what she did, and there's nothing we can do about it."

"Oh, c'mon," Channy said. "I know you like to play it cool, but you have to have an opinion."

Bon wiped sweat and a few strands of hair from his face, then leaned back on his heels and stared at her. "You don't care about my opinion. You're trying to get me to talk about Triana, either because you're upset with her, or because you're trying to get some kind of reaction from me about her. I'm not a fool."

"And neither am I. I don't know why you have to act so tough, Bon, when we both know that you have feelings for her. And, if you ask me, you had feelings for Alexa, too. Did you ever stop to think that it might be good for you to talk about these feelings, rather than keep them bottled up inside all the time?"

"And why should I talk to you?"

"Because I'm the one person on the ship who's not afraid to ask you about it, that's why."

"You're the nosiest, there's no question."

Channy slowly shook her head. "If I didn't think it would help you, I wouldn't ask. I'm not here for me, you know."

"Right."

"I'm not. I just want to help. The two people on this ship that you had feelings for, and they're both gone, just like that. Why do you feel like you have to deal with it by yourself? Are you so macho that you can't—"

"Please put the light back on the recycler."

"Forget the recycler!" Channy said. "Have you even cried yet? I cried my eyes out over Alexa, and I'll probably end up doing the same for Triana if she doesn't come back soon. You won't talk, you won't cry." She paused and leaned towards him, a look of exasperation staining her face. "What's wrong with you?"

He stared back at her with no expression. After a few moments, she tossed the flashlight to the ground, stood up, and stormed off down the path to find Iris.

Bon looked at the flashlight, its beam slicing a crazy angle towards the crops behind him. His breathing became heavy. For a moment he glanced down the path, his eyes blazing. Then, with a shout, he slammed a fist into the plastic covering of the recycling pump, sending a piece of it spinning off into the darkness. It wasn't long before he felt a warm trickle of blood dripping from his hand.

2

A chair toppled over and dishes scattered across the floor, producing a startling crash that pierced the calm, early morning air inside the Dining Hall. Shouts punctuated the noise. Lita, sitting alone in her usual seat in the back of the room, propping her head up with one hand and neglecting the breakfast before her, bolted upright. A knot of crew members near the door rushed to break up the fight, which had materialized seemingly out of nowhere.

The two combatants, at first separated by a handful of friends who'd been nearby, broke free from the restraining arms and lunged at each other again. They twisted into a furious mass of wild swings before falling in a heap on the ground, where they continued to wrestle and jab while astonished onlookers again scrambled into the ruckus, attempting to pull them apart. Two more crew members fell to the ground in the effort, and another chair went skidding aside.

It had all happened in mere seconds, instantly transforming a rather serene setting into a boisterous melee. The shock of it kept Lita in her seat at first, trying to absorb what she was seeing, before she sprang into action. Leaping to her feet, she raced over to the tangle of bodies. One of the boys had managed to position himself above the other.

"Stop it!" Lita yelled over the shouts, dropping to her knees and helping to drag the boy away, even as he lashed out with more punches. In the pandemonium Lita felt his elbow strike a glancing blow against her cheek, momentarily stunning her. At last the two were separated again, and Lita stood up between them with her hands outstretched on each of their chests.

"Enough!" she said. "That's enough!" She found her own breathing was coming in fits, matching that of the two crew members who stood poised, prepared to rush at each other again. Lita turned to one of them and narrowed her eyes. "Errol, what is this? What are you doing?"

The rugged boy from Scotland had a thin line of blood dripping from his nose, and a dark bruise had already formed near his chin. "Taking care of some long overdue business, that's all," he said.

Lita looked around at the other boy. He had recently completed a work rotation in Sick House, and she recalled that his temper had seemed short at times. It made this altercation less surprising. "You wanna explain this, Rodolfo?"

The Argentinean was also bloodied, but the cut near his right eye seemed worse than it probably was. He stared past Lita into Errol's face. "Just tired of his attitude, that's all. Tired of putting up with it."

"Attitude?" Lita said. She looked back at Errol. "Overdue business? Would you both listen to yourselves? I don't care what started this, and I don't care if you never speak to each other, but this will not happen again, understood?" She turned back to Rodolfo. "We've been through a lot lately, and the last thing we need is for you guys to do something stupid like this. This crew needs to come together, and not react by collapsing into chaos." She looked at the mess of food and plates on the floor. "Both of you, clean this up and get out of here. Then go back to your rooms and clean yourselves up. And stay away from each other until you can behave like adults."

For a few moments the two boys glared at each other. Lita gave a disgusted snort and walked back to her own table. Sitting down, she looked back to see Errol and Rodolfo slowly gathering the plates and utensils from the floor and setting the chairs back on their feet. The entire incident seemed surreal, a frightful glimpse into the dark turmoil that resided just beneath the fragile surface of their mission. Up until now there had been scattered incidents of disagreements and rare threats of violence. Suddenly the violence was real.

Lita, already weary from a lack of sleep the night before, and now troubled by this altercation, again rested her head on one hand. She wondered what might come next.

For a department labeled Engineering, its looks were deceiving. Unlike the stereotype portrayed in movies and television shows from the early days of the space age, it was not an expansive room filled with enormous turbines or stories-tall banks of equipment. If anything, it most closely resembled a compact series of laboratories connected by offices and storage rooms.

The majority of ship functions were under Roc's control, which left the crew to primarily monitor the operations, and to perform physical maintenance and updates. Vidscreens peppered each room in Engineering, along with computer terminals and work stations. The department included separate rooms for life-support functions, *Galahad*'s solar sail and ion drive systems, and information storage.

There also was a room devoted to the ship's defense. Unlike traditional defensive systems that utilized weapons, *Galahad* relied upon scanning devices that probed the path ahead. Contrary to a popular misconception, space was often anything but empty. A series of shields protected the ship and its precious human cargo from the deadly radiation which permeated the cosmos, as well as from potentially lethal debris.

A chief concern of early space exploration, the original long-distance vessels employed panels filled with water to block and absorb the radiation. *Galahad*'s designers knew that it was crucial to shield the crew, but, given the size and complexity with which they worked, water was not a realistic choice. Instead, scientists developed a magnetic shield which wrapped itself around the shopping-mall-sized ship and acted much like Earth's own magnetic field. That field, which generally went unnoticed and unappreciated by a busy human population, made its presence felt through its effect on compasses, and the showy delight of the aurora borealis. The Northern Lights were nothing more than Earth's magnetic field in a dramatic dance with the sun's highly charged particles.

As *Galahad* raced outward from the Kuiper Belt at speeds that were rapidly approaching the speed of light, a protective magnetic blast shot ahead, diverting toxic radiation out of the way, clearing a path. Because it clearly was one of the most crucial elements of the ship's defenses, crew members rotating through the Engineering section during their work tours were taught to monitor and maintain the radiation shield.

Ruben Chavez pulled up a chair and punched in his personal identification code at the work station. He'd finished a late afternoon workout in the gym, quickly showered, and reported to Engineering for a long stretch of work. After taking a personal day to catch up on some school assignments, he was making up work time in the radiation section, monitoring the forward scans. A few feet away, Julya Kozlova hummed while she charted the progress of a maintenance scan.

"What is that song?" he said to her. "It sounds like something my mother used to sing."

Julya smiled and, rather than immediately answering, turned to him and began to sing the song, adding words to the melody that she had been humming.

He closed his eyes, nodding to the beat, but then chuckled. "Well, that's no help. You're singing in Russian; that version probably wasn't a hit in Toluca."

"Hmm, you're probably right," Julya said. "But it's a traditional Russian love song; how it ended up in Mexico is beyond me. Perhaps your mother was more continental than you gave her credit for."

"Uh, no," Ruben said, laughing again. "It's more likely that the melody just happens to sound like the Mexican lullaby that she sang when my sisters and I couldn't fall asleep."

"How many sisters?"

"Four. Yes, four girls surrounding me, teasing and torturing."

"Made you tough."

He shook his head. "You have no idea." He bent over the console to pull up a tracking program, and allowed Julya to once again concentrate on her task.

The silence was shattered by a quick succession of tones that rang out from the room's main panel. After a pause, the sequence repeated. Ruben and Julya exchanged a quizzical look, then both stood and walked over to the display.

"That's odd," he said. "It's coming from the radiation control system."

"Running a diagnostic right now," she said, her fingers flying across the keyboard. She looked up at the monitor, then entered another command.

Together they watched as a response flashed across the vidscreen, then again looked at each other. "Uh, Roc?" Ruben said. "Are we reading this right? The diagnostic says the radiation shield went down for a second."

"Less than a second," Roc corrected. "But yes. I'd say *Galahad* just hiccuped."

"So we were completely vulnerable," Julya said. "That's one deadly hiccup."

Ruben scanned the monitor again. "Well, it seems fine now. But it can't really be fine, not if it's throwing off an alarm like that. *Something's* wrong."

"Correct," the computer said. "I hope you didn't want to spend this evening with a good book or crossword puzzle; this isn't exactly the kind of problem that you want to flare up again. Let's call Mr. Lee."

Julya nodded and punched the intercom to hail Gap.

Toward the end, Alexa had called it "our spot." It was the first time in his life that Bon had ever had someone reference "our," or "us," and he'd not responded to her. Instead, he had simply said,

"I'll see you in the clearing." To him it conveyed everything that needed to be said.

He stood now in that same spot, a small clearing tucked back within a secluded section of the dome. Night had descended upon *Galahad*, which meant the lights had automatically dimmed in an attempt to replicate a traditional twenty-four-hour Earth cycle. In the ship's domes that meant the artificial sunlight, which bathed the crops in a specially designed blend of ultraviolet and visible light, had faded away. It also meant that the brilliant nightly display was in full effect, a stunning shower of starlight through the dome's clear panels.

It meant nothing to Bon at the moment. He'd worked late in the fields, helping with the harvest of spinach—backbreaking work that he refused to skip out of merely because of his role as a Council member—before investing another hour in the never-ending pile of records and paperwork in his office. When he decided that a fourteen-hour workday would have to suffice, he fled not to his room and a waiting bed, but rather this garden-like patch that held a collection of painful memories.

Channy's words from the previous night still haunted him: *The two people on this ship that you had feelings for, and they're both gone.*

More accurately, two people that he had failed to share his feelings with. Both Triana and Alexa had given him every opportunity, and yet he had balked at the chances. Why? Because he was afraid to let down his guard, terrified of showing any sign of vulnerability? Was he subconsciously worried that he somehow wouldn't measure up, that they would ultimately decide that he wasn't worthy of their time and attention?

His mind drifted back, touching on the two occasions when

he and Triana had been close. Their brief connection in the control room of the Spider bay had lasted less than a minute, but long enough to make it clear that something existed between them, something worth exploring.

It was the second time, however, when they might have taken a step in that direction, that tortured Bon the most. Here, in the lush crops of *Galahad's* farms, not too far from this spot, it was a private moment that had irritated and confused him, and a scene that had replayed in his mind countless times. A quick, impulsive kiss from Triana, followed by a curious rejection when he responded. At the time Bon's anger had flared, and he walked away. He could still hear the words he spit at her that day: *You need to figure out what you really want.*

And yet, looking at it through a lens of time and perspective, he understood that it was he, not Triana, who wrestled with what he wanted. It was he who seemed to waffle back and forth, at one point open to the idea of their connection, the next unsure and distant. Triana might have given off a similar air of uncertainty, but now he felt sure that it was merely in defense of her own heart, a shield to protect herself until he was willing to meet her halfway. Her appeal to him at that moment—*This isn't the right time*—suddenly came into focus, and he saw the wisdom in her words. It had nothing to do with the ship's crisis at the time; it was Triana's acknowledgment that she was open and ready, willing to be vulnerable . . . but that he was not.

Triana, it seemed, was teaching him something about relationships, the necessity of two people being courageous enough to risk their hearts in order to meld. Teaching him, even now, across the winds of time and the depths of space.

He fell to the dirt and stretched out on his back, pushing his long, blond hair out of his face and then lacing his fingers behind his head. Staring up at the stars, and yet seeing nothing, he thought of the choices he'd made with both Triana and Alexa. If given the chance to go back and do it over again, what would he do differently?

Could he do things differently? Or were people hardwired to behave a certain way, with tendencies embedded within their genetic makeup, where no amount of conditioning or experience could alter their path? Bon thought of all the times that he knew—from experience—the right thing to do, and yet some stubborn side of him refused to go along. If that was truly the case, what did that say about the old adage of "learning from our mistakes"? Did we? he wondered. Did we really?

Despite his doubts, the fantasy of reliving the past year, of making different choices, forced itself upon him. He imagined an alternate history where he reached out to Triana, not merely in response to her, but through his own actions. What might have come of that?

Moments later his thoughts shifted, and he was here, in the clearing with Alexa, only instead of acting cool and detached, he responded to her gentle approach with openness and warmth.

She had deserved no less.

He closed his eyes and felt a wave of despair wash over him. This was a foolish waste of time, an exercise in futility. Alexa was dead, her body knifing through the void of space. Triana was gone, swallowed by a wormhole, and while the crew hoped for the best, the prevailing mood was that she was gone forever; Gap had gone so far as to begin the steps to replace her as Council Leader.

There was nothing he could do.

Or was there?

He sat up, leaned to his left, and shoved a hand into his right front pocket, grimacing as he raked the damaged skin of his knuckles. He pulled out a small metallic ball, studded with four rounded spikes that protruded from various points along its surface. He rolled the ball in his hand, staring at it through the gloom, wondering.

A minute later he was once again stretched out in the dirt, the ball lying beside him. His breathing turned deep and steady. Soon he was asleep.

3

The last thing Gap wanted was to walk into the auditorium after everyone was seated. In his mind it would seem arrogant, with an almost regal touch to it, and that was not the impression he wanted to make. Instead, he made sure he was the first to arrive for the meeting. With the large room to himself, he sat quietly in the first row, contemplating what the next hour would bring. It was the first full crew meeting of *Galahad* without Triana at the helm, and it already felt awkward. He was sure that it would remain so for quite some time.

His mind raced through the quick outline he had sketched. The talk would be direct and to the point. Given the crew's uneasiness, it could easily drift into an endless circle of speculation, with questions that sought reassurance more than detailed facts. It was his job to keep things on track and to deliver a measure of confidence that things would be okay.

But would they be? During its first year en route to Eos, *Galahad* had stumbled through its share of trouble, flirting with disaster several times. In some ways, the unnatural was a natural way of life for the crew. Now their Council Leader had disappeared, swallowed by a hole in the fabric of space that not even the ship's computer, Roc, could completely understand. And, compounding the shock, news of Triana's jump through the wormhole came before the crew had recovered from their first funeral.

And it was Gap's job to make this crew feel . . . confident?

He sat forward in his chair, elbows on knees, and stared at the floor. Now he understood firsthand the responsibilities of leadership. Triana had shouldered those responsibilities from the first day, with no whining, no wavering. In fact, it was a heavy feeling of responsibility that had driven her to climb inside the metal pod and venture into the unknown, at the risk of her own life.

Gap's task, he realized, paled in comparison.

A door to the auditorium opened, admitting a half dozen crew members and shaking Gap from his thoughts. A moment later Lita walked in, spotted him in the front row, and took the chair beside him.

"Need help with anything?" she said.

"Not that I can think of, but thanks." He sat back and looked closely at her. "You look pretty beat."

Lita laughed. "That's the nicest thing anyone's said to me in a long time."

"Oh, c'mon, you know I didn't mean it that way. You just look like you could use some sleep."

"Like most of us, I think. Plus, the stress of these last few weeks is starting to show up in a way I haven't seen before with this crew." She spent a minute catching him up on the fight in the Dining Hall.

Gap nodded grimly. "Everyone's stressed out and tired, no

doubt. But we can't start falling apart." He forced a hopeful look. "Who knows, maybe the fight let off some steam and things can settle a little bit."

"Maybe," Lita said, but there was a tinge of doubt in her voice. They both fell quiet for a moment and watched as the door opened and a dozen crew members strolled into the room.

Gap used the distraction to change the subject. "Have you given any thought to . . ." He paused, then finished in a low voice. "To who might take Alexa's spot?"

A crease appeared across Lita's forehead. "A little bit. On one hand I feel like I should tap someone pretty soon, just to keep a sense of order, you know? But then I wonder if maybe that wouldn't show the proper respect for Alexa." She shrugged. "There's no real reason to hurry; we're handling everything we need to so far. I think the crew on duty in Sick House are more worried about how to act around me. I don't like the feeling that everyone's walking on eggshells."

Gap nodded. He glanced over his shoulder to watch more crew members file into the room. The background noise picked up, which, in a way, put him more at ease. He looked back at Lita. "The way I figure it, the sooner we can get back into something that at least resembles routine, the better. Acknowledge the issue, answer the questions we can, and let the crew know that the mission doesn't stop, which means *we* don't stop."

Before Lita could respond, they were greeted by Channy, wearing what was likely her most subdued T-shirt. She took the seat on Gap's left.

"Where's your little furry friend?" he said to her.

"Stretched out across my bed like Cleopatra, sleeping. She probably won't move more than two inches before I get back."

"At least someone's getting some sleep around here," Lita said. "I'm jealous."

The room was now filled almost to capacity, the only empty seats caused by crew members on strict duty schedules. They would monitor the meeting through the vidscreen system throughout the ship. One of the last people to walk into the auditorium was Bon. He took a seat beside Lita, with merely a nod to Gap; he seemed to ignore Channy, who looked the other way.

"What happened to your hand?" Lita said, moving to lift Bon's hand from his lap.

"It's nothing," Bon said, pulling his arm away. "Part of the job."

"It looks gnarly. Stop by Sick House and let me swab some disinfectant on it, okay?"

Bon looked away and leaned back, his body language insisting that the conversation was at an end.

After allowing the room to settle, Gap stood. Lita gave his forearm a brief squeeze and mouthed to him, "Good luck." He climbed the steps to the stage and, grasping both sides of the podium, looked out over the crowd.

"Well . . ." he began, then paused for a few seconds. He felt a single drop of perspiration form along his brow, but refused to wipe it away. "I'm sure there are ten different flavors of the facts spreading around the ship, but here is the situation as it stands at the moment.

"As you know, the vultures, as we called them, fled the ship when we administered an oxygen blast to their leader. Rather than simply circle our ship, they left this part of space through an opening that we believe is a wormhole. Some might say that the vultures were summoned by their creators; we don't know for sure, but it seems the likely explanation."

He shifted his stance and looked back and forth across the room. Nobody moved or made a sound.

"What followed next is now clear. These . . . creators . . . opened another wormhole in our path. Why? We don't know for sure. But Roc speculated, and Triana agreed, that it was an invitation. An invitation for us to plunge through and pop out . . . somewhere else."

For the first time there was a stirring in the crowd. Gap saw crew members exchange looks, and knew that more of an explanation was due.

"We've all heard theories about wormholes, but we're the first humans to actually witness them. You can think of them as shortcuts across space, and perhaps across time. It's taking us years, using the most advanced technology ever devised on Earth, to travel a relatively short distance. With wormholes, travel across the galaxy, or across the universe—or maybe even between universes—would be instantaneous.

"Triana obviously believed that if we did not steer *Galahad* into this particular wormhole, there was a chance that something would eventually come out after us. Given this belief . . ."

Here, Gap paused again and collected himself before continuing. "Given this belief, Triana made a decision on her own, without consulting the Council, Roc, or anyone else. She gathered the corpse of the vulture that we had brought aboard . . . the one that was responsible for Alexa's death . . . and loaded it onto the pod we recovered from the Saturn research station. Then, she climbed inside, launched the pod, and took her cargo into the wormhole."

He looked down at Lita, who, although seeming on the verge of tears, offered him a supportive nod.

"That was almost three days ago. Since then we've scanned

every bit of space around us, and there's no sign of the pod. And, since the wormhole closed up soon after Triana's launch, we are now convinced that this is indeed what happened. She's gone."

Now Lita wasn't the only one in tears. Gap could see several crew members dabbing at their eyes. He steeled himself and continued.

"We've called this meeting for three reasons. One, to make sure you understood exactly what's happened; two, for us to discuss what happens next; and three, to answer any questions you have. Before we discuss our next steps, are there any questions so far?"

At first there was little response. The assembled crew members looked around, wondering who would be the first. Finally, from the middle of the room, a boy stood up.

"Yes, Jhani," Gap said.

"Do we have any idea if Triana could even survive going through a wormhole?"

Gap took a deep breath and weighed his answer. "We can't know anything for sure," he said. "However, I've had a couple of conversations with Roc about that very question, and he believes the answer is yes. He bases that on the limited data that we were able to gather from the captured vulture. Its physiology was obviously quite alien, and mostly artificial. Yet it also contained an organic brain—or, at least what we assumed was a brain.

"So," he continued, "if the vultures are able to navigate their way through wormholes unharmed, without any special protection that we know of, then we can assume that Triana would do the same. The pod that she was in is pressurized and very strong, at least as strong as the body of the vultures, which would hopefully provide the protection she needs."

Another crew member stood up. "Angelina," Gap said.

"Any ideas about what might be on the other side of the wormhole?"

Gap shook his head. "That, unfortunately, is something we couldn't even begin to guess. Our first thought would be the home planet of the vultures' creators, but who's to say they even live on a planet? Or that they're anything like us? And, if the wormhole comes out in a completely different dimension, we can't begin to guess about the laws of physics there. But, again, simply going by the physical makeup of the vultures, we would hope that it's at least habitable." He paused, then added, "I, for one, am counting on Triana coming back to tell us all about it."

This was greeted with hopeful smiles from around the room.

"Are there any other questions before we move on? No? All right, then let's talk about what comes next. Specifically, what do we do about the Council? As I said, I would very much like to believe that Triana will come back and everything will be fine. However, we also think it would be irresponsible to not take steps in case . . . well, in case she doesn't make it back anytime soon. We're in a tough spot, and it's crucial that our leadership be in order.

"As I'm sure you remember from your training and studies, according to the ship's bylaws, should *Galahad's* Council Leader be unable to fulfill the duties required—and that would be the case here—then the Council, in an emergency session, will meet to name a temporary Council Leader. That has happened, and, for the time being, the Council has asked me to assume those responsibilities, and I've agreed. However, it *is* temporary. The bylaws also state that an election should be held to replace the Council Leader, as quickly as possible."

There was a ripple of movement throughout the room as these words sank in. Just days ago it would have seemed unthinkable that they would be electing a new Council Leader. There were more glances and pockets of whispered conversation.

Gap raised his voice to refocus their attention. "I'll let Roc discuss the bylaws which govern this decision. Roc?"

The computer's voice, which eerily mimicked that of his own creator, Roy Orzini, spilled out of the room's speakers. While humor and sarcasm often dotted his speech, for this occasion he came across as all business.

"The bylaws for *Galahad*'s Council include sections that deal with emergency changes. In normal circumstances, members serve three-year terms, after which elections are held to either re-elect Council members, or install new ones. The Council was specifically set up to not resemble a hierarchy; no Council member automatically assumes the position of Council Leader should that Leader be incapacitated or otherwise unable to fulfill the duties. In this regard it's similar to the Supreme Court of the United States, where a new Chief Justice is appointed rather than having one ascend to the top.

"However, given the circumstances, this election also essentially falls under the category of a temporary fill-in position, although it could potentially last two years until the next general election. That means should Triana return in one month or six months or one year, she would resume her role as Council Leader, provided that she was able to fulfill the duties as established by the other Council members. Are there questions at this point?"

There were none, and Roc continued.

"The process is fairly simple. Nominations are submitted during a twenty-four-hour period via ship-wide electronic posting, either by the candidates themselves or by another nominating party. Then there are public forums over the next six days where the candidates may address the crew, and the following day an electronic election is held. No minimum percentage of votes is required; in other words, the highest vote-getter is named the new Council Leader.

"This new Leader will assume the role until the following general election, at which time they may run for re-election if they wish. Assuming no other problems, those elected two years from now will see the mission through its arrival into the Eos system."

From the stage Gap watched his fellow crew members absorb this information. He saw Channy lean over and mutter something to Lita, who nodded. Bon sat with a stony expression across his face.

After about a minute, Gap thanked Roc and once again addressed the crew. "We will open the nominating period tomorrow morning at six. It will last twenty-four hours. We ask that you take this responsibility seriously, and give it strong consideration before you randomly submit a name. Please speak with that person before doing so, to eliminate any discomfort or confusion. Once the twenty-four-hour period ends we will post all of the nominations.

"If there are any final questions, now would be the time before we close this meeting."

A low rumble spread across the auditorium as crew members spoke to their neighbors. Then, from the back row a girl stood up.

"Yes, Kaya," Gap said.

"I think most of us are under the impression that you have a good chance of moving into the top spot. Hypothetically, if you were the only person nominated, would there still be an election?"

Gap smiled. "Believe it or not, we would still have to have a formal election to install a new Council Leader. So, yes, even if only one person is nominated, we would all still need to vote. But let's not make any assumptions right now; there are obviously many people who would be well-suited to take over Triana's duties, and you should consider each person thoroughly."

He shifted again. "There are two things I'd like to add before we dismiss. First, keep in mind that you're electing someone who will have tremendous responsibilities heaped upon them. This is not a popularity contest, but rather an election to find the person we feel could best lead in times of trouble.

"But secondly, I'd like to point out that this crew is strong. We have overcome every obstacle thrown into our path, and will do so again. Our mission is to take this ship to Eos, to let nothing stand in our way, and to battle through any crises that may occur. We didn't train for almost two years in order to handle smooth sailing; we trained in order to confront, and overcome, any problems that came our way. Dr. Zimmer insisted that we be prepared for emergencies; well, that's exactly what we're facing now."

He took a deep breath. It was difficult to tell what effect his words were having upon the crew, whether or not they were encouraged and motivated. At the very least he knew that he had their complete attention.

"It's imperative that we pull together," he said. "You no doubt have heard about an altercation that happened this morning. That's the last thing we need. Emotions are wearing thin, but we need to think before we act out. We all have our assigned responsibilities, but this would be a good time to look around and see if we can lend a hand in other areas. That might very well help to relieve some of the tension. Please continue to find time to relax and decompress, but also keep your eyes open for ways you can help out. Thanks very much."

With a respectful silence, the room began to clear out. Gap stepped down from the stage and stood beside the other Council members.

"I thought that went very well," Lita said to Gap. "Thoughtful questions from the crew, and you handled it all very smoothly. Good job."

"Thanks," Gap said.

"And Kaya's right," Channy said, lightly punching his arm. "You're sure to get nominated. In fact, I'll be the first to do it tomorrow morning."

"Thanks again," Gap said. "But I don't believe I'll be the only one. There's been enough turbulence in the last couple of months that I'm sure someone else will step forward. But that's good, it's the democratic process at work."

"We'll see," Channy said. She leaned over and gave him a quick peck on the cheek, waved good-bye to Lita, and sprinted up towards the door. She had again completely ignored Bon, which Gap noted. He could tell from Lita's expression that she had as well. The Swede didn't appear to react at all, and, with a grunt of good-bye, trudged away.

Lita turned to Gap. "A little Council friction?"

"Well, those two seem to go through cycles, so I wouldn't worry about it."

Together they began the march up towards the exit. "You're probably right," Lita said. "So what's on your agenda for the rest of the day?"

"I've got some catch-up work to do in Engineering," Gap said, "but I think I might actually grab a quick nap first. I'm exhausted from the last few days. What about you?"

Lita sighed. "I need to settle on a choice for Alexa's replacement, so I'll be going over some crew records."

Gap put an arm around her. "I'm sorry. Need some help?"

She shook her head. "No, but thanks. Go get some rest. Maybe I'll see you at dinner tonight."

They parted ways in the hall, and Gap turneds towards the lift. He hoped that sleep would come easier now that the meeting was behind him. But his mind replayed what Kaya had said, and a new thought forced its way in: Am I ready for that job? Do I even want it?

4

The interview had gone swiftly and smoothly, and now Lita, who was rarely in the Conference Room outside of Council meetings, sat alone. Alexa's roommate, Katarina, had sent a note asking for a chance to meet—Lita knew it must be something about Alexa—so they had agreed to connect in the Conference Room. The interview had wrapped up early, so with time to kill Lita allowed herself to sit back and fall deep into thought, absently tapping her cheek with a stylus pen. Her gaze settled upon the room's lone window, and the brilliant star display brought on an emotional reaction, one that had a strong connection to her past.

As a child, she found herself intrigued with the stories of history's great explorers, most notably the famous Spanish explorers who struck out across the Americas. Enchanted by their gallant successes, and sobered by the lessons of their failures—including their often-disgraceful treatment of the natives they encountered—Lita grew to respect the heavy burden of responsibility that accompanied true exploration.

Now she was a Council member on the greatest mission of exploration the human race had ever conceived. In her mind, *Galahad*'s legacy would be judged not only by what they accomplished scientifically, but by how they represented their species morally and ethically. So far, in the first year of their mission, they had already crossed paths with two extraterrestrial entities. Whether they were technically life forms might be debatable, but for Lita that didn't matter. She was dedicated to making sure that *Galahad* did not repeat any of the blunders that her Spanish heroes had made.

She studied the star field and wondered how many other intelligent life forms populated the galaxy. And, of those, how many held moral beliefs that matched hers? It dawned on her that Triana's fate rested with the moral standards of the beings who waited at the other end of the wormhole; how did *they* treat encounters with an outsider?

So many questions, so many concerns, one of which had brought about the just-concluded meeting: who would move up to take Alexa's spot as her top assistant in the Clinic? Mathias was one of the final candidates, as was Manu, who had helped out during Alexa's surgery. Lita had earlier met with Mathias, and now had just finished an hour-long meeting with Manu.

Even through the mild-mannered veil he projected, Lita had sensed his intense desire for the position. More a conversation than an interview, he had impressed her by steering their discussion into hypothetical medical scenarios. His thoughtful suggestions, the questions he raised, and his obvious abilities displayed during his time in Sick House placed him squarely at the top of the list.

One of his questions stuck in her mind. "Suppose that Triana does pop back out of another wormhole," he'd said. "Without knowing where she's been, and what she's been exposed to, do we automatically let her back into the ship, or do we quarantine her?"

Her knowledge of—and fascination with—those early Spanish explorers made this question resonate strongly with her. Many historians believed that European diseases had decimated millions of native people in the Americas. Now Manu was suggesting that Triana might unknowingly carry an alien bug that could rage through the crew of *Galahad* before anyone knew what was happening. Lita found herself nodding in agreement when Manu spoke of the possibilities.

As much as her natural instinct would be to immediately embrace her friend upon arrival, Lita knew that Triana would have to remain isolated until thoroughly examined. Although, given its alien nature, would they even know what to look for?

And, just as sobering, how realistic were the chances that Triana would ever return?

Lita appreciated the respectful manner in which Manu had approached the subject; he knew, like every other crew member, how close Lita was to Triana. He'd also expressed sincere heartbreak over Alexa's death. Loss upon loss, as he'd put it.

Loss upon loss. Lita stared out at the fiery star display and, not for the first time, willed herself to not cry.

The door opened and Katarina stuck her head inside the Conference Room. "Still a good time?" she said.

"It is," Lita said, waving her in and gesturing towards the chair directly across the table. "Just taking a mental break." She laughed. "Although these days mental breaks seem to do more harm than good."

Katarina gave an empathetic look. "I feel the same way. As

long as I'm at work, or in school, or just busy with something, I'm focused and in control. It's when I'm alone with my thoughts that I get really sad."

"We'll probably all feel the same way for a while," Lita said. "Listen, I know I've told you this already, but if you ever just need to talk, or need a distraction, I hope you'll call me or stop by. You know that, right?"

"Yes, thank you. Really. And the same goes for you, too."

"I appreciate that," Lita said.

They sat in silence for a brief moment until Katarina placed a small box on the table between them. "This is why I wanted to meet with you," she said. "As weird as it might sound, Alexa and I once talked about what we should do if the other one . . . well, if something happened to the other. I don't think either of us really believed that anything *would* happen, but it . . . I don't know, it was just one of those late-night sessions, sitting around the room, talking. You know how it is."

Lita offered a sad smile, but didn't say anything.

"Anyway," Katarina continued, "it was almost like something out of a movie. We checked off a list of things we would leave for each other, and then we each wrote down what we would leave to other people on the ship. Kinda like our last will and testament, you could say."

Because space was at a premium in the housing section, crew members had been allowed to bring very few personal items aboard. Lita had given little thought to distributing her own possessions should anything happen to her. But now she smiled, because it was no surprise that Alexa—orderly and thoroughly efficient Alexa—would have planned for such a possibility and mapped it out.

"Alexa wanted you to have this," Katarina said. She pushed the box across the table. "You meant the world to her."

Lita hesitated. There was such a finality to this gesture, driving home the point that Alexa was gone for good. Finally, she reached out and lifted the small box from the table. Removing the top, she peered inside.

It was beautiful. Nestled within white tissue paper, it didn't shine; in fact, if anything, its charcoal color seemed to absorb light. Lita pulled the oddly shaped nugget from the box and twisted it in her fingers.

Katarina saw the look of curiosity and said, "It's part of a meteorite. Dug up in Antarctica about a hundred years ago."

"Where did Alexa get it?"

"Her mother gave it to her just before the launch. Told her that it was a gift from her real father."

Lita set the dark-gray rock on the table. "She never knew her real father."

"That's right, and her mother never spoke about him. I think that's why this was so special to her." Katarina looked from the meteorite to Lita. "Alexa told me that her mother thought it might make a great necklace, but you know Alexa. She never wore jewelry of any kind. So, she was holding on to it, trying to decide how to display it. And that night, when we were talking about things, she told me that you should have this because you *definitely* could make something cool from it.

"And," Katarina added in a soft voice, "you were one of her very best friends. She really looked up to you."

Another sad smile crossed Lita's face. She picked up the rock again and studied it. About an inch in diameter and heavy for its size, it was oddly smooth on one side, while cratered and worn on the other. She visualized its path through the solar system, one small piece of a much larger boulder that had likely spent billions of years tumbling through space, until either gravity or a chance impact had sent it on a collision course with Earth. It reminded Lita of the deadly ring of debris that *Galahad* had recently navigated; indeed, this particular chunk might have been part of the Kuiper Belt at some point. Or, possibly a fragment of a planetary crust, perhaps Mars, blasted into space as the result of a cosmic collision with a comet or asteroid. It arrived as a fireball, blazing through Earth's atmosphere, until it slammed into Antarctica. Now, ironically, it was once again tearing through space; this time, however, it was headed in the opposite direction, out of the solar system, a passenger on a starship.

"I think Alexa's mom was right," Lita said. "I think it would make a gorgeous necklace." She thought quietly for a moment, then said, "A couple of people on the ship have made their own jewelry. Yes, I think I'll get right on that."

Katarina smiled at her. "I can't wait to see it." She pushed back her chair and stood up, and Lita did the same.

"Thank you so much," Lita said, walking around the table to give Katarina a hug. "I will treasure this always."

When she again was alone in the room, Lita picked up the rock fragment and looked out the window.

"Born in the stars, and now returning to the stars," she mumbled to herself. "Just like us."

It would be agony. Yet agony mixed with . . . euphoria? Bon couldn't describe it, but that was nothing new. From the first moment he'd connected with the ancient life form labeled the

Cassini, he'd been at a loss to explain the feelings that coursed through his body and his mind whenever he tapped into their consciousness.

For that was essentially what he was doing: establishing a direct link with an alien intelligence that had flourished—and apparently had migrated throughout the galaxy—for a billion years. First discovered by a scientific outpost, the Cassini enveloped Saturn's orange moon, Titan, in a weblike network. Bon's brainwaves were aligned in a pattern that provided two-way communication with them, allowing the Cassini to plunder his mind, while at the same time providing an access point where the *Galahad* Council member could make requests and extract information. A portion of that information had secured safe passage through the deadly minefield of the Kuiper Belt.

The connection was established through the use of a device that scientists on the doomed outpost had created. Known simply as the translator, the small metallic ball opened the pathways between Bon and the Cassini.

The price of that connection was measured in pain. Bon's initial links with the Cassini had literally forced him to his knees, crippling him with agonizing spasms that brought him to the brink of unconsciousness. And yet, as time went by, and as more connections became necessary, he developed a tolerance for the excruciating pain, along with an understanding of how to maintain a touch of self-control.

And, he was forced to admit, he had also acquired an intense curiosity about it all.

Triana had become alarmed by Bon's sudden infatuation with the connection. She compared it to an addiction, a compulsion to link with something that might be causing serious damage.

Because of that, Triana had chosen to keep the translator in her possession. However, in a final meeting with Bon before slipping through the wormhole, she had left the translator with him. Had she done it intentionally? Bon couldn't be sure. But, in the days that followed, he'd wrestled with the responsibility; he *wanted* to connect, and yet Triana's words held a measure of power over him. The truth was, he couldn't be sure if his agonizing connection with the Cassini was an addiction or not.

One thing, however, was certain. There were questions he desperately wanted answers to, and the Cassini seemed to be the only reliable source of information.

He stood alone in Dome 1, a satchel strung over his shoulder. With this section of *Galahad*'s farming area deserted, Bon could hear a faint whisper of artificial breeze slipping through the nearby leaves, and an occasional tick from the automatic irrigation system. They were calming sounds for the boy who had been raised in a farming family.

He reached into the satchel and removed the translator, careful to not grip the device too firmly. He stared at it for a moment, absently dropping the satchel onto the dirt. Even in its inert state, Bon believed that he could feel the translator's power simmering within.

He had reached his decision earlier in the day. Triana's warning of an addiction echoed across time, but he rejected it. To concede her point would be to admit that he lacked self-control; this connection tonight, he told himself, was rather an exercise in *taking* control.

Beyond that, he'd spent much of the day getting clear on what the exercise was really about in the first place. Did he believe that it would work? Did he believe in the science behind it?

Did he even want it to work, or had the guilt imposed a feeling of obligation?

His strict, rational mind battled all of these questions until he found a relative place of calm acceptance. The connection itself with the Cassini would work; the results remained to be seen. A murky cloud concealed the validity of the science involved, which left him only his brief history with the alien force to go on; what they could—or could not—accomplish was impossible to know.

And the very fact that he was obsessed with the question in the first place convinced him that he did indeed want it to work.

He dropped to his knees, a position that he could assume either voluntarily or be forced into from the pain. Dropping the metallic ball to the dirt, he sat back on his heels for a moment, his eyes closed, and breathed in the moist air of the dome. He could feel his heart rate automatically begin its inevitable climb, and concentrated on the deep breaths that prepared him for the link.

At the same time, his mind sifted through the questions that raged within. He wondered if his ability to control the pain had advanced to the point where he could successfully frame the questions properly; when it came to dialogue with the Cassini, Bon was most certainly the infant talking with the parent. It was best to prepare as well as possible before attempting the conversation.

A shout from across the dome caused Bon to open his eyes and cock his head to one side. He didn't want company during this episode. But the voices that drifted through the fields moved off in another direction.

With one final long exhale, he reached out and loosely picked up the translator. Then, shifting it to his palm, he closed his grip.

Immediately his head shot backward, his entire body racked with pain. An instinctual cry slipped from his mouth and his teeth clenched. The breathing which had been slow and smooth just moments earlier was now labored and fitful. His shoulders twitched with spasms that seemed to be tearing around inside his body, racing from point to point. His eyes rolled back before closing, and brilliant orange light splashed across the insides of his lids.

Sounds began to seep from his mouth and soon coalesced into a small symphony of voices. It signaled an extension to a small group of other crew members who came close to sharing the same neural patterns as Bon. They would not be aware of the connection, yet would find themselves suddenly battling headaches.

Nothing, however, compared to what Bon was feeling.

After a few seconds his conscious mind began to fight the overpowering presence of the Cassini, pushing back their grasp. He had learned to rein in their ravenous appetite for control, to somehow maintain a sliver of his own identity while they buzzed through his head. It stemmed the tide of pain somewhat and allowed him to focus his thoughts.

His eyes fluttered open briefly, long enough to assure him that he was still alone in this patch of the dome. Then, with a force of effort, he pushed a thought into the forefront of his mind and fought to keep it there, as if demanding to be heard. He would compel the Cassini to hear him.

Rather than a steady torrent, the pain began to pulse through him in waves. There were moments where it dissolved to nothing, but then rushed through again, sending him back on his heels. During one of the breaks, he caught his breath and transfered the thought into words.

"Where . . . is . . . she?"

When the opportunity presented itself, he asked again.

And again.

5

Who doesn't love a good magic trick? Even when it's something as simple as pulling a coin out of someone's ear, people don't want to think about how the magician palmed the coin, or how they fooled everyone into looking this way while they focused over there.

No, deep down, what you humans really love about magic is the surprise. It's almost a challenge, in a way; you know that you're being manipulated, but you always believe you're sharp enough to spot the misdirection. Then, when the trickster pulls it off, you almost have to laugh.

In fact, that love of the unexpected shows up in many forms, and always seems to bring a smile. Surprise parties, finding money in a coat pocket, or when an old friend shows up out of the blue . . .

Wait. That last one can often be the biggest surprise of all.

Gap picked at his dinner, his usual hearty appetite taking a break this particular night. The Dining Hall was still fairly busy, especially given the late hour, but Gap sat by himself, a vidscreen open before him.

He went over the data again—he'd lost track of how many times now—and yet nothing about the blip in the radiation shield made sense. He stabbed at an apple chunk and was lifting it to his mouth when he stopped.

Hannah Ross stood before him, a tray in her hand.

They stared at each other for what seemed an eternity, until Gap slowly set down his fork. "Hi," he said.

"Hi. Mind if I sit down?"

Gap's mind spun out of control. The two of them had been an item for a couple of months, but their breakup had not been pleasant. Since that time they'd not spoken at all, despite a few attempts by Gap; when Hannah had not responded, he'd given up. Now she stood there, asking to sit with him . . . and he froze.

There was no question in his mind that he would say yes, but how enthusiastically? Should he simply shrug, as if it didn't matter to him one way or another? Or should he smile and offer a pleasant welcome, without conveying excitement or nonchalance? What could she possibly want to discuss, anyway? Was she missing him? He certainly missed her, and it was good to—

"Well?" she said.

He mentally shook the sand out of his brain; he'd been staring up at her with his mouth halfway open. "Uh, yeah, sure," he said, indicating the chair across from him.

She sat down, bumping the table in the process, and Gap reached out to steady his water before it turned over. They both chuckled nervously, each aware of the awkward beginning. Hannah quickly began to arrange her tray, aligning the edges so that it paralleled the edge of the table. She set out a knife and fork, keeping them perpendicular to her, then placed a napkin on her lap. During the entire production she made no eye contact with Gap.

Once settled, she began to eat, taking a bite of salad, then re-setting her fork on the table, neatly aligned. She pushed her long, blond hair out of her face, only to have it fall back. She repeated the motion, this time tucking the unruly strands behind her ears.

After another quiet minute she finally spoke. "I hear there was some excitement with the radiation shield. What was that all about?"

Gap studied her face. So, he thought, this is all business. All right, he could match that.

"That's a good question. It lasted less than a second, but that's enough to set off the alarms. No reason that we know of." Then, not liking the way that sounded, he added, "At least not yet."

Hannah nodded. "I wondered if . . . well, you didn't ask my opinion."

Gap smiled at her. "Okay, I'll play. Hannah, what's your opinion?"

She took a bite of an energy bar and chewed thoughtfully before responding. "I was thinking about how many strange things we've come across already, and yet we're barely out of our own backyard. I'm sure we've all thought about what was on the other side of the wormholes."

"Yes?"

"And I wondered if maybe a completely different form of radiation might have leaked out before it disappeared."

Gap sat back and considered this. He had to admit, the idea was fascinating. Who could say what poured into or out of these portals?

"That's an interesting idea," he finally said. "And you think it might be a type of radiation that we're not equipped to filter out?"

"Maybe."

"Hmm," he said. "Well, I'll have a chat with Roc about that. Thank you. Anything else?"

Hannah fidgeted with the edge of her tray. "I've also wondered about the area of space that we're rushing into. As every second slips past, we're getting farther and farther away from the sun's protection. I mean, the Kuiper Belt was dangerous, but for all we know it's even more dangerous out here."

"And that danger might be radiation," Gap said.

"Right. We've always assumed that cosmic radiation would be fairly consistent throughout the galaxy. But perhaps our sun protects us more than we thought. Once we're outside that cocoon, it might jump drastically."

He nodded, but kept his gaze on her. It didn't take long for him to sense her discomfort.

"I'm sure you'll figure it out," she said. She took another bite, then a sip of water. Gap sensed that there was more she wanted to discuss besides the radiation emergency. But he waited patiently; she'd approached him, after all.

A minute went by before Hannah spoke up again. "I'm just sick thinking about what might have happened to Triana," she said. "It doesn't seem possible that she could be gone for good." For the first time since sitting down she looked into his face. "What does your gut tell you? Will she be back?"

Gap winced. "You know, I'm getting that question a lot. Everyone wants to know what I think will happen."

"Human nature," Hannah said. "During a time of crisis, we like to be reassured. Or at least given a glimmer of hope. That's probably where everyone is right now, just wanting to hold on to some hope that she'll be back."

"And what if she doesn't come back?" Gap said. "If I go around telling everyone that Triana will magically pop back out of nowhere, and then she doesn't . . ." He shook his head. "I can't do that. You have just as much information as I do, just like the rest of the crew. It's impossible to imagine what might happen. All I know is that we have to go with the assumption that she *won't* be back; then, if we're lucky enough to see her again, fantastic. But I don't know, and it's not smart to speculate."

She broke eye contact with him and peered at her plate of food. "I imagine you've given some thought to the possibility of being the new Council Leader. How would you feel about that?"

He paused, wondering what had prompted the question. Was *this* why she was suddenly talking to him again? Was she intrigued with the notion that he might become the ship's commander?

"I've thought about it," he said slowly. "But only because so many people have talked to me about it. It's not something that I even contemplated before Triana took off."

"Not ever?"

Gap looked away for a moment. "Well, I've thought about the automatic crew election that's coming up in a couple of years, whether I'd want to run for a spot on the Council again, or, if Triana wanted to step down, maybe the top spot." He looked back at her. "But I haven't dwelled on it, if that's what you mean."

She shrugged. "You and Triana have totally different personalities. What do you think you'd do differently if you were in charge?"

He sat back again and drummed his fingers on the table. "What's this all about?"

"What do you mean? I'm just talking with you."

"That's exactly what I mean. You've avoided me completely, haven't responded to my notes. Now suddenly you're talking with me like nothing ever happened. Like the old days."

Her gaze drifted back up to meet his. She put down her fork, dabbed at the corner of her mouth with her napkin, and took another sip of water. Again, Gap was patient.

"Maybe it takes me longer to get over things than it does for you," she said. "Especially when you were the one who ended it."

"I didn't end it," Gap said evenly. "I told you that I was going through a rough time and didn't think I'd be good company for a while. That's not the same as ending it completely."

"So it was my turn to go through a rough time then, okay? Maybe I wasn't good company for a while. Besides, you wanted your space, and you got it. It's not worth fighting over now."

"You're right, it's not. I'm just curious why suddenly you want to talk again."

"Would you prefer I leave you alone?"

He sighed, feeling exasperated. "No, I'm glad you're here. Sheesh, can a guy at least ask a question?"

Hannah sat stone-faced for a moment, and then a slight smile curled at the corner of her mouth. "Yes, you can. I'm just a little nervous, okay?" She winced and rubbed her leg. "I'll probably end up with a lovely bruise on my knee just from trying to sit down here with you, pretending to be calm."

Gap returned the smile. "For what it's worth, I didn't exactly put on a relaxed face either. When you walked up I probably looked like a fish in a net, gasping for air." He let them both enjoy the brief silence after their mutual acknowledgement, then said, "I'm sure that I would probably operate a little differently than Triana. Probably a bit more communication with the crew, just because of my nature. She's quiet, and I'm . . . well, I'm not.

"And," he added, "I'd probably want to look at crew work schedules, maybe tweak things a bit. I think we're starting to get a little rusty with some of the basic chores around the ship. I don't know if it's complacence, or if we're just tired. But after everything we've been through recently, I know that we need to be on top of everything. This radiation warning is just a reminder that, even though we're out of the Kuiper Belt and the vultures are gone, it doesn't mean we have smooth sailing ahead."

Hannah took another drink, set her glass down, then reached out and nudged it about an inch to the right. "The crew seems pretty comfortable with you, don't you think?"

It was funny, Gap realized, how things turned so quickly. He'd gone through a difficult stretch where his self-confidence was shot, where he felt that he was contributing next to nothing as a Council member, and had even contemplated resigning. Now, in a flash, he was on the brink of running for Council Leader. His esteem, in the eyes of the crew, had grown considerably since he'd unmasked the methods behind Merit Simms's plot to force a return to Earth. Was the crew comfortable with the idea of Gap as the ship's leader? Probably, he decided.

That still didn't mean that *he* was completely comfortable with the idea. He had to admit, however, that just hearing Hannah talk about it sent a charge through him.

Or was it simply the notion that Hannah might be impressed with him as Council Leader?

"I can't speak for the crew," he said. "I would hope that they'd be comfortable with anyone on the Council stepping up to lead."

A half-smile once again crept across Hannah's face. She took a last bite of her dinner—Gap noticed that she'd barely touched the plate of food; was she really here for dinner?—and slowly pushed back her chair.

"Well," she said, "I have some work to do before bed. It was good to talk with you."

"Yeah. Good to see you, too." He watched her drop off her tray and slip out the door. For the next few minutes he found it impossible to refocus on his work. Like the ship itself, his own shield had been briefly pierced.

And his own personal alarms were going off.

An hour later Gap made his customary nightly visit to the ship's Control Room. The scattered work stations were thinly manned at this late hour; *Galahad*, for the most part, was tucked in for the night. Three crew members nodded a hello to him as he walked in, and then settled back into their calibrations and reports. A faint stream of music trickled in from hidden speakers, and the large vidscreen displayed the almost hypnotic splash of stars. It was tranquil—one reason Gap never dreaded this part of his daily routine.

But he was also exhausted, physically and mentally. "Five minutes," he had promised himself on the walk from the Dining Hall. "Five minutes, and then to bed."

It didn't work out that way.

He had barely fallen into the chair at his station when the entire room was flooded by a blinding flash of light. It shattered the calm of the room like a billion strobe lights simultaneously firing outside the ship. Gap and the three other crew members instinctively threw their hands up to cover their eyes, but by then it was over. Looking down and away from the vidscreen, Gap blinked several times and shook his head.

"What was that?"

Gap looked at the girl who had asked the question, then stole a hurried glance at the vidscreen. Even though he'd not been looking directly at it when the flash came, it had been powerful enough to leave afterimage spots dancing across his vision. "I have no idea, Addie. That was . . . interesting."

He blinked rapidly again and turned back to his work station. "Roc, did we just witness a supernova or something?"

"Give me a moment," the computer said. "But no, it was not an exploding star."

While waiting, Gap quickly checked in with Engineering and was told that there was no change in the radiation shield. Whatever the light flash might have been, it hadn't caused damage to their defenses.

Not obvious damage, at least.

"This is quite odd," Roc said a moment later. "A flash that intense, and yet there is zero residue."

Gap chanced another look at the screen. "What do you mean?"

"I mean there's nothing there. I have a perfect fix on location, even approximate distance—not that far, by the way—and yet there's nothing there. No object of any kind, no residual radiation, nothing. It's as if it never happened."

"Ugh, tell that to my retinas," Gap said. "Good thing none of us were staring into the vidscreen at the time." He leaned forward and ran a hand through his hair. "So, first a failure of the radiation shield, and now a blast of light that came from nowhere. Anything at all that you can find?"

"The light was more than light," Roc said. "And I'm not trying to be funny. I mean, I don't need to try, it just comes naturally. But in this case I'm just telling it like it is."

"And I have no idea what you're talking about," Gap said.

"Good, because I don't either, and I'd hate for you to know something that I didn't. But essentially that flash was charged somehow. Not your standard light as radiation charge; more like a strange shower of particles. Or rather, a shower of strange particles."

"Why do you say that?"

"Because we have no data on these particular particles. Until two minutes ago, no human being—or ultra-cool computer—has ever witnessed them."

Gap looked again at the screen, prepared to quickly avert his eyes. The information tumbled through his mind: a blast of light, combined with mysterious particles, and all from an invisible source.

He would not be in bed in five minutes.

6

She stood with her hands clasped over her head, catching her breath, drenched in sweat. The sharp tang of salt stung her mouth, but it wasn't an unpleasant sensation. Quite the contrary; for Channy there was no better feeling than a strenuous workout, one that worked her lungs to the max and brought about a dull muscular ache that actually felt good. Today's cardiovascular drills had featured some of her favorite participants, crew members who relished the same intensity at least a couple of times each week. She thought of them as the race horses, thoroughbreds who bolted from the gate with a determination that never let up, never faltered. It was a test that no one in this particular group wanted to fail.

The gym shared *Galahad*'s lower level with the Airboard track, the Spider bay, and the Storage Sections. It was usually a beehive of activity during the morning workout sessions, and now, as crew members left to shower and grab breakfast, Channy began to plot a new exercise routine for the afternoon group. Her roommate, Kylie Rickman, her face splotchy and streaked with sweat, sauntered over and tossed a towel at *Galahad*'s Activities Director.

"You would make Einstein proud," Kylie said.

Channy passed the towel around her neck. "Einstein? What are you talking about?"

"He was the one who suggested that time was affected as you approach the speed of light. Well, as this ship gets closer and closer to that speed, your concept of time is getting skewed. Twice today you said 'keep it up, one more minute.' I timed it, and we went more than two minutes both times."

"Oh, it didn't hurt that bad," Channy said with a laugh. "Besides, you're not supposed to be watching the clock during my workouts."

"Just wanted to see if my time perception was screwed up, or if you're just a monster. News flash: you're a monster."

Channy rubbed her face with a corner of her towel, then picked up a cup of water. "You'll thank me when we get to Eos."

They both took swigs of water, then Kylie said, "So, what do you think of Gap as the new Council Leader?"

Channy laughed. "He hasn't even been nominated yet."

"He will be, you know that."

"Well," Channy said, "I think he'd do a great job. He obviously has the experience from being on the Council, and I think the crew respects him. Especially after that whole Merit Simms garbage."

"Speaking of Merit," Kylie said, "I heard rumors that at least one other person might be nominated from the crew. You don't think it'd be him, do you?"

"Merit?" Channy said. "Are you kidding? He wouldn't stand

a chance. He might get three or four votes from his circle of friends, but that's it."

Kylie shrugged. "You're probably right. I just can't think who else might run." She tossed her towel into a hamper. "All right, I'm off. A shower and then back to work. See you 'round."

Channy watched her roommate trudge towards the door, then stiffened as Bon passed Kylie on his way in. If he caught a glimpse of Channy he didn't show it, and instead made his way towards the exercise bikes. Never one to join a group workout, the Swede focused on solitary workouts with cardio machines and weights.

With a scowl, Channy eyed him for a few moments, resisting an urge to walk over and say something. She was still angry with him, and thankful that he mostly confined himself to the seclusion of the domes. On one hand she could appreciate why he loved it up there, why he felt so passionate about his work in the fields. He might be emotionally detached from people, she thought, yet maybe his connection to nature didn't allow those personal feelings to develop.

But she refused to feel sorry for him. After her own recent heartbreaking experience, she couldn't understand how anyone could allow a potentially beautiful relationship to slip through their fingers without fighting for it. She might have lost out in her pursuit of love, but she could hold her head high in the knowledge that she had given it everything she had.

Bon, for all of his gruff demeanor, had been too afraid to let down his guard with Alexa. Channy vowed to never wall off her heart like he had done.

As if on cue, he turned his head and briefly made eye contact. Then, simultaneously, he turned his attention back to the bike while Channy spun on her heel and stormed back to her office to finish the day's planning.

G ap had barely seen his room in the past week, except for quick sleep breaks. After lunch he forced himself to seek shelter there, to sit quietly and meditate for an hour. He dimmed the lights, dialed up low, soothing background music, then sat cross-legged on his bed and closed his eyes.

More than anything he wanted to calm his mind, and allow himself to process the events which had cascaded upon each other in the past few days. He hadn't even come to terms yet with Triana's surprising disappearance when suddenly he was confronted with the task of temporarily leading the crew. He had barely begun to acclimate to that duty when the question of his nomination as Council Leader was presented.

And now, before he could adequately consider that wrinkle, Hannah had suddenly popped back into his life, sending his thoughts pinwheeling out of control. Her questions, as well as her tone, seemed to imply that she was not only encouraging him to pursue the position, but that she had finally recovered from their break.

Did that mean she was open to the idea of reconnecting?

So many new complications, all within a matter of days. Not to mention the potentially deadly radiation threat, and now a mysterious bolt of space lightning. No wonder he felt overwhelmed and in need of downtime.

He craned his head to one side, then the other, and pulled his shoulder blades back. Even the stretching helped a little bit, and he made a conscious effort to control his breathing: deep inhale, hold, long slow exhale.

When he felt himself settling into a relaxed state, he began to address the matters one at a time. With Triana, there wasn't much within his control. She was gone, she might or might not return, and they were doing all that they reasonably could at the moment. He acknowledged that the primary issue with Triana was of a personal nature; his feelings for her were a mixed bag, including a new tinge of anger.

But none of that was helpful. Emotions might run strong, but his rational mind fought to put all of that behind him for now and to concentrate only on the relevant—and actionable— things on his plate.

Leading the crew for the short term didn't seem to be a problem. The nervousness that he felt at the beginning of the crew meeting had quickly evaporated, and it was obvious that he felt comfortable in that position.

Did that equate to taking on the position of Council Leader on a full-time basis? He had admitted to Hannah that the idea was appealing. A nomination was easy enough to come by; then it became a matter of convincing the crew that he was the right person for the job. He would easily have the support of the other Council members, including Bon, who would merely want the process over and done with as quickly as possible.

And he seemed to have the support of Hannah Ross. Why was that suddenly so important to him?

He knew that, of all the things on his plate right now, this was the least critical, and yet it had forced its way to the top. Since their brief meeting in the Dining Hall, he found himself not only reliving each moment of the conversation, but suddenly recalling many of the things they had done together months before. The feeling was not unlike the original sensation of their relationship, which on the one hand confused him, but on the other hand excited him. He'd questioned his role in their breakup so many times, and recognized that he regretted how he'd handled it all. Just the chance to make it up to her, to undo all of the hurt he'd caused . . . that's all he'd hoped for. It seemed like the door might have opened.

What would happen if he rushed through that doorway? He had to be honest with himself, and acknowledge that the idea of reconnecting with Hannah had certainly caused a jolt of excitement. For a few moments he allowed himself to daydream, to envision a future—perhaps a very near future—where he was suddenly *Galahad*'s Council Leader, and Hannah was once again at his side. All would be forgiven, they would work together, they would laugh together . . .

Was it too good to be true?

His thoughts were interrupted by the voice of the ship's computer.

"So sorry to burst in like this," Roc said. "But there are a couple of things we need to talk about right away."

Gap opened his eyes. "What's up?"

"First, just to satisfy my curiosity, how do you sit like that without your feet falling asleep? And second, our little blip with the radiation shield has happened again."

"What? How long this time?"

"About a second and a half, and then all seemed normal again. *Seemed* would be the operative word. Things are not normal, and they're getting less so with each passing hour. Engineering has gone on alert. Ruben was around again this time; I told him I would let you know."

Gap pushed himself up from the bed and slipped his shoes on. "Tell Ruben I'm on my way, and let the other Council members know, would you please?"

He sprinted out the door, and two minutes later rushed into the Engineering section. The air felt charged, and all eyes immediately turned to him. Ruben was waiting.

"Same as last time," he told Gap, and together they hurried over to the radiation control panel. "An alarm went off, and this thing lit up like crazy. The first time it barely blinked; this time it was still quick, but lasted a little longer."

Gap looked over the data, then, using the keypad, fired off a sequence of code. "Roc," he said while he typed, "are we able to isolate whether it's an internal issue with our shield, or if it's being caused by something from the outside?"

"Now *that's* an excellent question," the computer said. "If this is what happens when you sit in that lotus position, I won't make fun of it ever again."

"Roc . . ."

"Well, let's just say that I haven't been able to isolate any particular malfunction with the unit itself. However, that doesn't mean the failures aren't affecting it. And, since we've run tests on the ship itself and found no cause for this, it might be time to see what's going on outside. I see you're setting up an external scan."

Gap shrugged. "It's the only thing that makes sense. If the system had a problem it would show up in one of the diagnostic checks. Hannah brought up the idea that something might have leaked out of the wormholes."

Ruben, who had been standing quietly behind Gap, spoke

up. "But the wormholes have all closed up. Why would they affect us now?"

"I don't know," Gap said. "Maybe they're not. But it's an interesting theory." He finished typing in the code, then stood back and looked up at the monitor. "And, even if that's not it, we might find that it's something else out there. We're definitely in uncharted space now; who knows what we'll run into?"

He ran a hand through his spiky hair. "Now, Roc, let's talk about something you said a few minutes ago. You said the system is getting less normal. Explain that."

"One drop in the shield was fine, especially for less than a second. Now, with multiple drops I've picked up a fractional decrease in unit efficiency."

Ruben gave Gap a confused look. "What does that mean?"

Gap exhaled a long breath. "A fractional decrease in unit efficiency sounds like a fancy way of saying that it's wearing out."

"Not fancy," Roc said. "Sophisticated. 'Wearing out' is so . . . common. But it works out to the same thing."

Gap understood immediately and considered the possibilities. One particularly nagging thought forced its way in, but he didn't want to vocalize it in front of Ruben and the other crew members who stood nearby.

If it was an external problem, it was apparent that the ship's defense shield had problems with it. Big problems, which were getting worse with each incident. And if they couldn't be remedied—and quickly—then all of the other things he'd thought about in his room wouldn't matter at all. *Galahad* would be a lifeless shell, hurtling through space.

7

He'd insisted that Roc wake him by five thirty, for the day was sure to be interesting. And yet when the ship's computer pulled him from a dark, heavy slumber with an imitation yodel, Gap groaned and pulled the pillow over his head.

Roc immediately piped in sounds of a rooster crowing, letting it repeat three or four times.

Gap pulled a corner of the pillow away from his mouth. "Hey, Daniil doesn't need this, you know. At least let *him* sleep."

"Your roommate left ten minutes ago for an early morning workout," Roc said.

Turning over and raising himself up on one elbow, Gap saw the empty bed on the other side of the room, then fell back. "How does he do it?" he said under his breath.

"Willpower, determination, a sense of pride," Roc said. "If you need help looking those up, I'll help you with the spelling."

"You're not as funny as you think you are," Gap said, letting the pillow fall back over his face.

"Oh, really?" the computer said. "Is *this* funny?" Suddenly the room was filled with the sound of screaming monkeys.

After enduring it for half a minute, Gap sat up. "All right, all right, I'm up."

The sound of monkeys was replaced with the soundtrack of applause. Despite his irritation, Gap found himself laughing. "Okay, I'll admit, that's funny."

He stretched and hauled himself to his feet. The next few minutes were spent showering and getting dressed for the day. By six o'clock he was sitting at the computer, scanning his mail and checking reports from the ship's various departments. His first priority was the update from Engineering; with a sigh of relief he saw that no further radiation shield breakdowns had occurred overnight.

Just before falling into bed he had sent a note to Bon, requesting an update on crew work schedules. There was no response yet.

The other item that tickled at the back of his mind would be posted on the crew's message board. He glanced at the clock in the lower corner of his monitor, saw that it was almost 6:15, then punched in the key to take him to the main board. Highlighted against the random messages that were tacked there was a bulletin from Roc; it was tagged *Council Leader Nominations*.

He sat back, his finger hovering above the Open key. A strange sensation swept over him, and it took a moment to realize that it was a combination of two separate fears: one, that he would not be nominated, and two, that he *would* be nominated. He took a deep breath and silently acknowledged that both scenarios held equal amounts of tension. If his name was on the list, it meant that he was one step closer to taking on responsibility for the most daunting mission humankind had ever embarked upon.

If his name was absent, it meant that the crew found him undeserving.

He couldn't bring himself to open the bulletin. The seesaw battle within him began to rage again, beginning with the swirl of anxiety that he was unworthy of the role. His earlier self-doubts bubbled back to the surface, the same doubts that had plagued him weeks ago and had slowly been put to rest.

At the same time he found that deep down he craved the validation from his peers. He'd worked hard, beginning at the *Galahad* training complex, and during the first year of the mission. This, in essence, was what he had spent the last two and a half years of his life working for.

He drummed his fingers on the desktop for a moment, then leaned forward and clicked the Open key. His eyes quickly scanned the notice from Roc:

The twenty-four-hour nomination process, in which every crew member was eligible to submit a name as a candidate for the position of *Galahad* Council Leader, has officially ended as of six o'clock this morning. Two crew members have been nominated, and will now face an election in one week.

Gap immediately seized upon the two names listed in alphabetical order. The first one was Gap Lee.

Below it, the other name glared out from the screen, searing both his eyes and his heart in one shot.

Hannah Ross.

He sat, frozen in his chair, barely breathing. No matter how long he stared at the name, it didn't seem real. Slowly he pushed back his chair and stood up, but kept his gaze locked on the screen. His mind drifted back to his conversation with Hannah in the Dining Hall, and within seconds he felt a surge of anger.

She had quietly quizzed him about his plans, all the while aware that she would be a competing candidate for the position. She had tricked him, he was sure, into opening up and spilling his thoughts about the position itself, as well as his intentions for the crew.

And now she was going head-to-head with him in a run for Council Leader of *Galahad*.

He began a relentless march around the room, hands on his hips. Each time he passed his desk his eyes darted back to the taunting name on the screen.

Hannah Ross.

He silently fumed. Suddenly it was no secret why she had broken her long stretch of silence. He had allowed himself to sit there and entertain wispy daydreams of rekindling their relationship. He had imagined them once again laughing together, walking hand in hand, holding court like a royal couple aboard the ship. How could he have been so blind, so foolish? How could he have . . .

Wait, he told himself. What about her? How could *she* have done this to *him*?

He stalked to the far side of the room and leaned with one hand against the wall, the other running through his hair. Then, with a loud exhale, he rushed back to the computer, closed out of the bulletin board, and snapped off the screen.

In seconds he was out of his room, storming down the deserted corridor, with no particular destination in mind.

* * *

A t eight o'clock the lower level of *Galahad* was bustling with activity as crew members passed each other in the hall, some heading towards the gym, others winding back to the lift after finishing a workout. They exchanged boisterous greetings, many punctuated with friendly jabs. There were also excited conversations exchanged regarding the bulletin board posting about the upcoming election. The chatter lent an excited air to the gym side of the ship's basement level.

In the opposite direction things were much quieter. Tucked around a corner from the lift was a corridor that led to the Storage Sections and Spider bay. Shrouded in mystery, the Storage Sections had been sealed before being loaded onto the ship, with explicit instructions that they not be touched until reaching Eos. The Spider bay was *Galahad*'s hangar, housing the sleek metal shuttles that would eventually carry all of the crew members to the surface of one or both of the two Earthlike worlds that orbited the target star.

Along this hallway was a large window that framed a spectacular cosmic display. Hannah stood there now, leaning against the wall and gazing out at the fiery array of stars. She instinctively picked out the familiar constellations, mentally cataloging the individual stars of which they were composed. Her mind skipped through their descriptions, everything from star-type to size to distance from Earth. Growing up in sparsely populated Alaska she'd been blessed with a sky free of light pollution, allowing her a beautiful canvas upon which to gaze, and which later inspired her to create dazzling artistic renditions of cosmic scenes.

None of which could compare with this view.

She understood, however, that the exercise of naming the stars was purely a distraction from the anxiety which gnawed at her. It had, in fact, been eating away at her for a full day. By now she was sure that Gap had seen the announcement of her nomination; she was also quite sure of his reaction.

Ironically, this had been the location of some of their most intimate conversations. Huddled together, gazing at the spectacle outside, this had been the setting for her happiest moments. They were moments she'd never forget.

Nor, for that matter, would she likely forget the transformation within her that was born from their split. She wondered if the change would have occurred anyway, at some given point in her life, but needed the kick-start that Gap had unexpectedly provided. For the most part she felt as if she was the same Hannah as before—her devotion to science, her need for order, her outward manner, for instance—and yet a subtle shift had definitely taken place. Her decision to accept the Council Leader nomination was merely the first public evidence of that shift.

Now she traced a finger along the pane that separated her from the icy vacuum of space, and—although she knew it was only her mind playing tricks with her—felt that same cold flowing through her body. Her stomach was in knots.

The nomination had not been her idea. In fact, when originally presented, her initial response had been to laugh and politely decline. But the more she listened to the crew member sitting across from her in the empty Conference Room, the more she had been seduced by the possibilities, and by the logic of it. A fresh viewpoint, a fresh voice, a new direction. It had somehow made sense.

Now that she had seen her name on the screen, the magnitude of it weighed upon her. This meeting with the crew mem-

ber who had nominated her was, if anything, a pep talk designed
to steel her nerves for the weeklong campaign ahead.

She heard the footsteps but kept her face glued to the window. A moment later she heard him speak.

"I'm guessing you didn't eat anything this morning." The
voice had a tinge of laughter behind it.

"Ugh," she said. "I don't want to think about food right now.
My stomach won't be able to handle anything for a while."

She felt him slowly approach and stand beside her, staring out
at the stars.

"I will never, ever get tired of this view," he said.

She nodded in reply. They remained silent for a moment before turning to face each other. Merit Simms pushed a strand of
long, jet-black hair out of his face and offered a smile.

"So, other than the butterflies, how are you feeling?" he said.

Hannah shrugged. "Okay. Nervous, obviously."

He turned his head slightly and frowned. "You're not second-
guessing this, are you?"

"No. Well, maybe a little. But it's done, and I'm ready to move
forward."

His crooked smile returned. "Good, I'm glad to hear that."

Hannah looked into Merit's eyes and, not for the first time,
questioned the tenuous connection she had formed with him.
She reminded herself that it was only a few short weeks ago that
Merit had led a movement to virtually overthrow the Council
and, in so doing, turn the ship around and return to Earth. It
was Gap who had discovered the treacherous methods to which
Merit had stooped, including sabotage. The entire plot had been
revealed to the crew in a dramatic showdown in the auditorium,
and, from that moment on, Merit had receded into a shadow of

his former blustery persona, becoming practically invisible on the ship.

Until now.

He pulled a step closer to her and placed a hand on her shoulder. "You're gonna be a great Council Leader. You're exactly what this crew needs right now."

Hannah looked down at his hand, then slowly back to his face. She noted the faint scar beneath his right eye, and the dark, thin hairs on his chin. A moment later he slowly withdrew the hand.

"Listen," she said, stepping back to re-establish the distance between them. "We touched on this once, but I want to make sure that we're clear on one thing. I'm not doing this as part of some personal crusade that you're waging against Gap."

Merit's face twisted. "Of course not. All I said was that you're gonna be great, that's all."

"I know what you said, but I also know that you're carrying around a lot of bitterness towards Gap. I'm just telling you that this has nothing to do with your issues with him."

"I don't know what—"

"We're not debating this right now," Hannah said. "I've said what I needed to say, and we can move on."

Merit tried unsuccessfully to rein in a smirk. "Good. I think the next order of business is making sure that you get in front of the crew right away, so they can start to get comfortable with you."

Hannah stared back at him, then shook her head. "What is this?"

"What do you mean?"

"I mean that you sound like . . . like some kind of campaign manager or something. That wasn't part of our discussion."

"I told you that I would be happy to help," Merit said. He

leaned against the wall opposite her and crossed his arms. "Hannah, I came to you because I think you'd be a great choice as *Galahad*'s Council Leader. You understand, probably better than anyone, what's going on out here in the void, and the crew respects you because of your sharp mind. On top of that, you bring a fresh approach to things. But you've never done anything like this before, and it wouldn't hurt to have some friends helping out."

Hannah chuckled. "So now we're friends?"

Merit looked down for a moment, then pushed off from the wall and faced her. "Why don't I just let you handle everything on your own? You suddenly don't want anything to do with me, that's obvious. I don't know if you're just overwhelmed with the reality of the situation, or if you really hate me that much. But all I did was nominate you because I thought you'd do a great job, and then offered to help. Sorry if I wasted your time."

He turned and began to walk away. Hannah hesitated, then quickly reached out and grabbed his arm.

"No, wait a minute," she said.

It was his turn to look down at her hand. When she pulled it away, his gaze tracked upward to her face. "Well?" he said.

Hannah looked away for a moment. "I just need everything to sink in, okay? I'm sure . . ." She paused, taking a couple of deep breaths. "I'm sure that I'll have questions for you. And . . . thanks. I appreciate your offer to help."

Merit pushed a strand of hair out of his face again. "Don't freak yourself out over this, Hannah. Don't make it more overwhelming than it needs to be."

She smiled weakly. "I tend to do that with things."

"Everything will be fine. We'll talk, we'll map out a strategy that you're comfortable with, and then let you roll. Hey, if you lose you don't get thrown off the ship or anything. What's the worst that can happen? You lose an election, maybe, but you earn a pretty respected place on this ship. So stop worrying. The crew will still love you no matter what."

He flashed a quick smile, then walked away, back towards the lift. In a few seconds Hannah was alone again, near the observation window. She let out another deep breath, then leaned against the window and peered out.

"It's not the *whole* crew I'm worried about," she whispered.

W*hen motion pictures were first introduced, it wasn't unusual for the audience to yell at the movie screen. People were so captivated by the drama unfolding before them, they felt that they could holler and the actors would hear them and react.*

I get the feeling that's exactly what some of you are doing right now. Listen, you can yell at Hannah all you want, but she can't hear you.

And even if she could, it might be drowned out by other little voices screaming in her head. My recommendation is that you at least wait and see what develops between Hannah and Merit. It might turn out fine.

Of course, it might also be disastrous.

Besides—and be honest—how many times have you really listened when people tried to warn you about something? Just like you, Hannah must take the path of her own choosing.

8

The decision had weighed heavily upon her, but Lita felt confident of her choice. Certainly both Mathias and Manu were qualified, but only one of them would be her new top assistant; the other would be disappointed. She had developed friendships with each, so it pained her to know that one would be dealing with an emotional setback. But it was simply the way it had to be.

She quickly checked her e-mail, then left Sick House and made her way to the Conference Room, where she found Manu already waiting.

"Prompt, as always," she said, smiling at him before grabbing a cup of water and taking a seat.

"My dad was big on making a good impression," he said.

"You've certainly done that." She sipped at her water, then leaned forward on the table. "I won't keep you in suspense, Manu. I just spoke with Mathias a little while ago. He's been a terrific member of the Clinic team, and was a strong candidate for the position. But I've decided to offer you the spot, if you're still interested."

He beamed at her. "Absolutely! Wow, that's great. Thank you."

"You've earned it," she said. "Now, just promise me one thing."

"Name it."

"Remember all of those questions you asked during the interview? Well, don't stop asking them. In fact, I want you to work on answering a few of them, too."

Manu sat back and looked thoughtful. "I have one question right now, if that's okay. It's a bit personal."

"I'm sure I can handle it."

"Well . . . since we started talking about this, I've thought about what happened with Alexa. I wasn't there the day it happened, and I guess I'm just wondering . . ."

He seemed unable to finish the sentence. Lita volunteered.

"Wondering how you would handle a life-and-death situation on the ship?"

He nodded. "Yeah. I'm not worried about any of the work that we're doing, and I know I could pretty much handle an emergency situation when it comes up. But how exactly do you prepare for . . . that?"

Lita rubbed her forehead and considered the question. "You don't prepare for it."

He looked confused. "What do you mean?"

"I mean that the medical training that you had before we left, and the extra work you've put in during the first year, will give you the knowledge you need to handle the situation. But I don't think you can mentally prepare for the worst."

She paused, and her mind instinctually drifted back to conversations she'd had with her mother. Maria Marques had tried to condense her many years of medical experience into several short lessons for her daughter, helping Lita to understand not the book knowledge necessary for *Galahad*'s five-year voyage, but rather the psychological strains that a ship's doctor would need to manage. During her toughest incidents since the launch, Lita found that she often fell back on those intimate discussions with her mom.

Maria had faced her own share of professional crises, one in particular which was personally devastating. Although it affected her on many levels, she maintained her devotion to her calling and served the medical needs of her hometown in Mexico, fighting her way through the personal pain. It was a lesson that Lita clung to during her most trying times.

Now, she stared across the table at Manu, and once again reached back across the mind-numbing distance to her home by the sea, to her mother's wisdom and love. She offered a smile and said, "Nothing that you do to prepare yourself for that moment will ever replicate the actual emotions that you'll feel when it happens. All you can do is wait and see how you're built for it. You can't read about it, you can't do any exercises to train for it, and you can't learn from someone else; you have to experience it, and then learn from it. Hopefully you'll be able to apply it the next time it happens."

Lita stopped and tried to gauge Manu's expression. He seemed to be processing everything that she was saying. He nodded, just a slight dip of his head, and pursed his lips.

"I see what you're saying. I just hope that I handle it as well as you did."

Lita lowered her head, ashamed that he would see the truth in her eyes. Afraid that he would look inside her and reach a different conclusion, one that she felt stained her somehow. A long silence followed.

Finally, she looked up and tried one more smile. "You'll be fine, Manu. I know it."

In her heart, she hoped that someday she would be, too.

The noise level in the Dining Hall had tapered off a bit, but Hannah still found it distracting. With her dinner tray neglected beside her, she glanced back and forth between the table's small vidscreen and her workpad, which was perfectly aligned with the table's edge. She would occasionally squint at something on the screen, then bend over her workpad and modify the figures that flew from her stylus.

Her ordered, logical mind worked best when left undisturbed, but that was impossible on this night. More than a dozen crew members stopped by, either before or after their meal, to wish her good luck in the upcoming election; she graciously thanked each of them. A handful of people sat down beside her for a moment to express their surprise at her willingness to campaign, given her shy reputation; at this, she could only offer a shrug. How could she explain something that she herself couldn't quite understand? But now that the dinner rush was waning, she settled into her work.

It was her mother who had first exposed her to the beauty and magic of puzzles. Some of Hannah's favorite memories as a child included long, cold nights in Alaska, curled up with her mother in a blanket on the couch, each of them furiously trying to solve a word or number puzzle. Often they would download the same puzzle, and then race to see who could successfully finish first. They each kept a bag of chocolate treats on the table before them—Hannah's favorites were the chocolate-covered macadamia nuts—and the winner could select anything from the other's collection. It added a new level of competition to what was already quite fun for Hannah, and from that moment on she was hooked.

The puzzle at this particular moment, however, had more riding on it than a piece of chocolate. The potential danger suggested by the brief failures from *Galahad*'s radiation shield was, in fact, deadly. For while space might appear empty, it teemed with high-speed, high-energy charged particles, moving at ferocious speeds. Each star's blast furnace spewed radiation into its planetary system, and the galaxy itself seethed in a lethal dose of cosmic radiation.

Earth's powerful magnetic field shields it from the majority of harmful particles. Generated deep beneath Earth's surface, in the molten iron that makes up the liquid outer core, this field effectively surrounds the planet. Radiation particles are diverted around Earth, repelled much the way a ship's bow pushes water to each side. *Galahad*'s defense system was designed to work in primarily the same fashion, using electromagnetic forces to bend and push the cosmic radiation to the side as the ship cut through the vacuum of space. Without this shield, crew members would quickly be subjected to deadly cell mutation and damage.

What's more, now it appeared that each successive jolt was causing extensive and lingering damage to their only defense. In a sense, a timer had effectively been started. When it ran out . . .

Hannah read and then reread her notes. She was juggling multiple ideas, a collection of possibilities that might explain the shield dilemma. Just as one idea would take center stage in her mind, she would find countless reasons why it didn't make sense. Then another idea would shift into the spotlight, to be analyzed and tested. Promising scenarios were filed away for later study, while others were immediately discarded.

She snapped the page on her vidscreen to the graphic supplied by Galahad Command prior to launch, the one which plotted the positions of the outer gas planets, the Kuiper Belt, and beyond. She furrowed her brow as she scanned the page. It had been impossible for the scientists on Earth to guarantee what the teenage crew would encounter this far out; the best they could manage, given their limited information, was an educated guess.

No humans had ever passed this way before. Hannah and her crew mates were pioneers.

She wondered if this stretch of space held the answer to the breakdown in *Galahad*'s radiation shield. Not within the shield itself, but something . . . out there. She turned her attention back to her notes, then to the screen, then the notes. Space, she thought; what is different about this portion of space compared to the billions of miles we've left behind? What has changed?

She rubbed at the sore spot on her knee and, glancing around to make sure she was unnoticed for the moment, rolled up her pant leg. She examined the purplish bruise which had blossomed there, a painful remnant from her awkward encounter with Gap and the table. "Klutz," she muttered to herself.

With an exasperated sigh, she sat back and tapped her fingers on the table. "Roc, have you got a second?" she said.

From the vidscreen's speaker came the computer's deadpan voice. "Well, part of me is assisting Lita with some crew records right now. Another part of me is tied up in Engineering, trying to iron out a bug in the artificial gravity grid; can't have someone walking down the hall and suddenly end up bouncing against the ceiling, now can we? Plus, there's a literature session going on in school right now, and I'm getting all sorts of queries about some guy named Twain. Oh, and the usual mundane requests from the remaining two hundred crew members, things generally not worthy of my vast intellect. I'm stretched like taffy. But for you, Hannah, I can easily spare a second. Maybe more."

She smiled. "Thank you for devoting a sliver of that magnificent brain to helping me. I'm wondering about this." She tapped the vidscreen graphic with her stylus, highlighting a section. "I've factored in the solar radiation at our back and the Milky Way's radiation hitting us straight on. I've even considered that we might be absorbing some form of radiation from your good friends, the Cassini."

"Hey, what do you know?" Roc interrupted. "The hotshot from Alaska tosses a joke. Who would have thunk?"

Hannah's smile returned; she had always envied Gap's unique relationship with the ship's computer, the easy manner in which they exchanged good-natured barbs while still maintaining a close working relationship. Although not exactly in her nature, she had wondered if her own relationship with Roc might expand if she adopted a similar approach.

"But none of that seems to add up," she said. "I mean, rather than an obvious outside influence, I thought it might very well be something about the basic properties of space. Would you agree?"

"Yes."

Hannah waited for more, but nothing seemed to be coming. "Uh . . . okay," she said. "Thanks."

"Sure. That was easy. And not much more than a second. Of course, my curiosity is piqued. You're assuming that the problem is, to put it delicately, a deformity in space. Am I reading you correctly?"

"Maybe," Hannah said. "Do you see where I'm going with this? And, if so, do you think it makes sense to keep checking it out? Let me know if you think I'm wasting time here."

Roc paused, and she could almost imagine his artificial brain flickering with activity before he answered, "I say continue."

She let out a deep breath. "Okay, great. Thanks again."

"That's why I'm here," Roc said. "And now, if you're finished with me, I have to help someone conjugate a verb in one of the romance languages."

Hannah again tapped her fingers on the table. She sighed, absently rubbed at the bruise on her knee, and let her mind begin its inevitable calculations. It might be a long shot, but it was at least something to explore. And it might—might—be the answer they needed to solve the radiation mystery.

Which ultimately might save their lives.

9

I know that I, like many of you, tend to get caught up in the whirlwind of activity that seems to swirl around Triana and Gap, and these days even Bon. But it's Lita who often catches my attention because of her thoughtful musings. You could almost say that she flies under the radar. When it comes to profound thinking, she's at the head of the class, in my opinion.

Dr. Zimmer had laughed when, during a training meeting, Lita announced that she had no intention of allowing *Galahad's* Clinic to "smell like a hospital."

And, to her credit, it didn't. She was adamant about keeping the disinfectant odor to a minimum, and made maximum use of the ship's storehouse of scents, any of which could be dialed up through the vents. This morning it was a calming hint of cinnamon.

She pulled up a chair next to the desk once occupied by Alexa. Manu was busily arranging things to his liking, including a photograph of his family. His parents, two brothers, and a little sister surrounded him in the image. He told Lita that it was taken during the crew's final visit home before the launch, which she silently accepted as the explanation for the sad smiles.

She had her own sad-smile family photo beside her bed.

She also couldn't help but notice what resembled a charm, dangling from a slim, dark chain. Manu had hung the charm from the edge of his vidscreen, but, although it didn't stand out as a display, Lita had no doubt that there was significance to it.

For almost half an hour they talked about Manu's new responsibilities. When they reached a natural break in the orientation session, which allowed them to stretch and relax for a minute, Lita said, "So, any questions so far?"

"After doing so much filing and record-keeping, do you almost wish for someone to come in with a scratch or twisted ankle?" Manu said with a grin.

"A doctor's life is rarely glamorous," she said. "But you'd never know that from watching the movies. Hollywood would never have survived showing what we really do most of the day: routine exams, doing a lot of reading and research, and filling out forms."

"But you love it."

"I do," Lita said. "I grew up around it, so the behind-the-scenes stuff didn't surprise me at all. It's just a matter of being ready in an instant; that's what all of your training is about."

Manu nodded. "My grandfather was a nurse and EMT. I guess there might be something about caregiving that runs in our blood."

That didn't sound far-fetched to Lita; she'd known of many families that had several generations somehow involved in medical practice. She'd never thought of the art of caregiving as a gene that could be passed down, but who knew? Once again Manu had stimulated her thoughts, another sign that she'd made the right decision.

Before diving back into their work, she glanced at the charm hanging from his monitor. "If I'm being too nosy, please tell me. But I'm curious about this beautiful charm. Is there a story behind it?"

"No, I don't mind you asking," Manu said. He lifted the chain and held it out to Lita, who gently held it in her palm while examining the polished stone it held. "It's an amulet."

Lita raised an eyebrow. "An amulet? Like a . . . good luck charm?"

He smiled at her. "In a way, yes. Amulets turn up in a lot of countries on Earth, and there's lots of different beliefs that go along with them. This one's Egyptian, and it's been in my family a long time. In fact, it belonged to that grandfather I told you about. He was raised practically in the shadow of the Great Pyramid, so he grew up bathed in the stories and traditions. He gave this to me when I was selected for the *Galahad* mission. Said I was taking the magic of the pharaohs with me to another world."

"And what belief did your grandfather associate with this?" Lita said, turning the stone over. The reverse side was marked with smooth scratches, obviously etched with a particular message in mind.

"He said it was created to ward off evil."

"Do you believe that?" Lita said.

Manu seemed to consider the question for a long time before offering a small shrug. "Let's just say it was important to him, and to his father, and on back. I respect *their* beliefs, even though

I haven't decided yet for myself." He took back the amulet when Lita held it out, and draped it once again over the vidscreen. "What about you? Do you believe in that kind of stuff?"

Lita leaned forward on the desk and crossed her arms. "For me," she said, "it's a question of faith versus fate. A lot of people see those as the same thing, but I don't."

"And how do you see the difference?"

"It's just my own opinion, of course," Lita said, "but I happen to think that faith involves believing in something that can affect what's going to happen, whether that's a supreme being or simply a higher power in the universe. Fate, on the other hand, to me implies that there can be no manipulation of what's to be."

Manu grinned at her again. "And which camp do you fall into?"

She gave a half-shrug. "I guess I'm a bit like you: still trying to decide. I'm grateful that I was brought up in a very tolerant and open-minded family. My parents taught me both sides and encouraged me to decide for myself which direction to go." After a pause, she added, "But let's face it, things happen as we go through life that make us sway back and forth between the two possibilities, don't you think?"

"After what's happened here, which camp are you in today?"

Lita started to answer, then stopped. It was a tough question, with a complicated answer. As much as she enjoyed the rapport with Manu and appreciated their talks, she wasn't sure she was ready to open up this much with him. This was, after all, supposed to be merely a training session; somehow they had drifted into very personal terrain.

Of course, she had started it by asking about the amulet.

"I guess I'm on the fence right now," she said with a smile. She sat back in her chair and hefted her workpad. Manu seemed to pick up the clue that it was back-to-work time. He sat up straight and punched a key to take the vidscreen out of hibernation mode.

For the next hour they covered more administrative territory, from crew data to pharmacy records to report filing. They ended the session with a cordial farewell and made plans to meet the next day for a refresher course on physical exams.

Lita glanced at the clock, noting the late hour. Getting Manu organized had been important, but now she had work of her own to finish, as well as a detailed summary to prepare for the next Council meeting. As enticing as sleep sounded at the moment, her responsibilites were piling up and demanding attention.

Except that Manu's question kept forcing its way back into her thoughts. Where *did* she stand on the question of faith versus fate? Were the two compatible? And what did it mean if she wasn't sure of her stance? She picked up the stylus pen from her desk and absently began tapping her cheek with it, her gaze drifting to Manu's desk. The amulet sat mutely on its chain, yet somehow seemed to beckon her.

Evil spirits, he'd said, guarded against for generations. She agreed with Manu about respecting other people's beliefs and traditions, but this was one belief that she could not share. She understood the value of customs or rituals that provided comfort, but her scientific mind was reluctant to embrace good luck charms; to her they fell into the category of superstitions.

Manu had said that he was undecided about the amulet's power, and yet she also got the sense that he was hedging his bet. The fact that he displayed it near his workspace suggested that he might be willing to believe. Lita was okay with that.

Besides, she reasoned, with the ways things had been going

lately aboard *Galahad*, a little bit of supernatural protection couldn't hurt.

Y ou haven't responded to my messages," Gap said, leaning against the door frame. With night officially blanketing the ship, he'd trudged through Dome 1 in the darkness, glancing up at the stars that filtered in from above, guided by the light that spilled from Bon's office.

The Swede kept his eyes on the desk vidscreen. After a long stretch of silence, he answered in a reluctant tone. "It didn't seem urgent. I've been busy."

"I came by an hour ago and couldn't find you. Most of the workforce has been gone for a while."

Bon finally looked up. "Should I check in with you at all times?"

Gap tried inserting a smile. "No. Maybe I'll just put a tracking beacon on you."

The humor seemed to have no effect on Bon, who turned his attention back to the screen. Gap slowly walked over and sat in the chair facing the desk, then tilted back onto the chair's rear legs. Now he was able to see Bon up close, and at once something jumped out at him.

"You're soaked in sweat. What in the world have you been doing?"

Bon's voice was laced with irritation. "I told you I've been busy. Is there something specific I can help you with?"

"Yes. I need to know if you got the message about the Council meeting tomorrow; it would be nice to get a response to that. Plus, I thought the message about crew rotation was pretty simple. Shouldn't have taken more than thirty seconds to answer that."

"Yes, I will be at the meeting. No, I'm not prepared to rotate for another couple of days."

"May I ask why, or is that too much?" Gap said.

"Because we're in the middle of two large harvests right now, and I'd like to keep some continuity until we're at least past the heaviest load."

Gap nodded. "Good enough. See how easy that was?" When he got no response, he added, "What's going on with you? I mean, besides the usual. I don't expect a spirited conversation when we chat, but there's something else these days."

Bon looked up again; this time Gap could see that his hair was matted against his forehead and appeared damp. On top of that, there seemed to be a slight tremor in his hands; faint, but there nonetheless.

"I get very weary of these verbal games," Bon said. "Why don't you just ask what you really want to ask?"

"All right," Gap said. He brought his chair back onto all four legs and leaned forward, his elbows resting on his knees. "You've been even more hermitlike than usual since we lost both Alexa and Triana. You've retreated into some sort of emotional cave, and now you're not answering messages. On top of that, you have the exact same look that I saw after one of your Cassini connections. Do you have the translator?"

"Yes."

"You've used it, haven't you?"

"Yes."

Gap felt a ripple of anger and took a deep breath to keep from lashing out. "And you felt like you could do that without discussing it with the Council?"

"Yes."

"Okay, enough with the one-word answers," Gap said. "Save us some time and talk about this with me. What are you doing with the translator in the first place?"

Bon sat back in his chair and crossed his arms. "Triana brought it to me before she disappeared. She made the decision to keep it in her possession, and then made the decision to give it to me. She *was* the Council Leader at the time, remember? She didn't have to get your blessing for everything that she did."

"Spin it any way you want, Bon, but you know that she couldn't ask the Council about giving that thing to you without giving away her plan to leave. That doesn't mean that you shouldn't have reported it to us afterward. And it certainly doesn't mean that you should just begin using it without discussing it with the Council. The thing is, you know that. And not only that, someone should be with you when you connect. Probably Lita."

"It doesn't affect me the way it used to," Bon said.

"Right. That's why you look like you've just run a marathon."

Bon shrugged but didn't respond.

Gap studied the face staring back at him. During the early stages of their *Galahad* training on Earth, he and Bon had developed a tenuous friendship—or at least the closest thing to a friendship of which Bon was capable. But the extreme differences in their styles and personalities had ultimately pushed them apart, and things cooled. A mutual interest in Triana furthered the split. They had settled into a cool but cordial working relationship, but the tension continually simmered underneath.

The next question was likely to evoke a vague response, but Gap knew that it was the only natural follow-up. "What did you talk about with the Cassini?"

Bon chuckled, but it was humorless. "Personal."

Gap shook his head. "Sorry. When it comes to that link, it can't be personal."

"Oh, really? According to who?"

"Like it or not, Bon, I'm the acting Council Leader, and I have responsibilities. Quit fencing with me on this."

"Quit pushing me," Bon shot back. "Yes, you're the acting Council Leader, whatever that really means. But I've paid my dues and then some when it comes to the Cassini. It was my link with them that got us through the Kuiper Belt, and it cost me. I don't think anyone would begrudge me a private connection now and then. Well, not most people, anyway."

"I see. So now you're calling in your chip as the ship's savior, is that right?"

"I didn't bring this up, Gap; you did. I don't feel like I've done anything wrong, nor anything that required the attention of the Council."

Gap pushed up from his chair. "Well, I hate to break it to you, but it has now come to the attention of the Council. And it will be on the agenda for tomorrow's meeting."

Again, Bon gave no response. He looked up at Gap with an icy stare.

"In the meantime," Gap said, "I'll hold on to the translator until the meeting."

"No."

The ripple of anger quickly became a torrent, and Gap found himself doing everything in his power to keep from exploding. He knew that he was essentially powerless at this point; he couldn't wrestle Bon to the ground and physically take the device. This round had gone to Bon.

"Okay," he said. "We'll discuss it tomorrow."

"Fine," Bon said. "Tomorrow." He lowered his gaze back to the vidscreen and resumed his work.

Gap seethed inside at the dismissal. He spun on his heel and quickly walked from the office, back into the gloom of the dome's night.

10

The fist landed with a dull smack against the side of Karl Richter's jaw, knocking him backward, but not off his feet. At first his eyes widened with shock, but they quickly narrowed as he stepped forward to close the gap between himself and his attacker. The three farm workers who had witnessed the punch were frozen in place, not believing what they were seeing.

"You don't seriously want another one, do you?" Liam Wright said. He held one cocked fist at his side, slowly pumping it up and down. "Now beat it."

Karl, the side of his face turning a dark shade, lunged. He wrapped his arms around Liam's midsection and drove him into the damp soil at the edge of the corn plants. Once on the ground, the boys' fury exploded. Arms and fists flailed with only occasional success as they rolled a few feet into the stalks of corn, snapping several at knee height. Their grunts and exclamations were muffled under the canopy of plants. Dirt flew as each tried to gain traction. In seconds Liam had Karl pinned to the ground and managed to connect with another blow to the side of his head.

Two of the farm workers, at last shocked into action, leapt into the fray and grabbed Liam's arm before he could do further damage. In turn, he swung wildly at both workers, which allowed Karl the chance to roll away and clamber to his feet. As soon as Liam looked back to find him, Karl stepped in and landed his own solid punch. There was a crack as Liam cried out and fell to his side.

Karl stood back, breathing heavily, wincing from the shots he had taken. He relaxed his tense muscles and dropped his arms. At that moment Liam flew upwards and grabbed Karl in a wrestler's headlock. Blood from Liam's broken nose began to spatter over both of them. They tumbled backward, a writhing mass, and then slammed into one of the field's irrigation pump units. The plastic shell on the unit cracked as it bent sideways, ushering a fountain of sparks and loud pops as it shorted out. The two boys collapsed over the ruptured pump. Karl let out an animal cry of pain.

By now the third worker who had been frozen in place jumped forward, joined by the two who had unexpectedly been victims of the fight. They again pulled at Liam, who this time voluntarily stepped back. The four of them looked down at Karl.

A shard of plastic from the crushed irrigation shell had punctured his right thigh. He rolled to his left in agony, revealing a fresh cascade of blood that soon saturated the ground.

The third farm worker stripped off his shirt and knelt down. He pushed Karl's hand aside and examined the wound, doing his best to wipe the blood away with the shirt. He turned to the others and yelled, "Get help! Hurry!"

While one worker sprinted away, Liam coughed once and

spat. He gingerly touched his nose and managed to smear blood across the side of his face. Looking down at the groaning figure on the ground, he said, "Is he okay?"

The worker turned to glare up at him. "As if you care. Why don't you get yourself up to Sick House? You've done enough for one day. Go on, get out of here."

Liam stood motionless, unsure, for several moments before turning and walking up the path. By the time he approached the lift he passed Manu and another Sick House worker, running in the other direction, each holding a first-aid bag.

Hannah couldn't understand why it was so difficult to recall memories from her younger years. A few things were imprinted, but there were large gaps. It was as if a firewall sealed off portions of her life, refusing to allow her access. She had casually mentioned it to Dr. Armistead during their training, without making a big deal of it. As the mission psychologist, Angela Armistead had been responsible for evaluating each potential crew member's ability to adapt to a long space voyage. The last thing Hannah had wanted to do was send up a red flag. And yet she was curious about why her mind behaved the way it did, and wondered if the dark spots in her memory were somehow tied in with her need for order and discipline.

"I know that pop psychologists like to automatically assume that you're blocking out some traumatic experience," Dr. Armistead had said at the time, offering a supportive smile. "That might be true in some cases, but I personally think that it's often merely a case of our brains maximizing their resources."

She went on to explain that each person was wired a little

differently. Some placed an emphasis on emotions or feelings, while others might be more likely to follow a routine of logic and reason; there was no correct way, no wrong way, just different ways. In Hannah's case, Dr. Armistead explained, she felt most comfortable with things in a proper sequence. It helped to explain Hannah's obsession with order and neatness, her need for items and objects to be strictly aligned, and her razor-sharp attention to detail. The fading of early memories was, quite possibly, her mind's way of organizing the most important and pertinent information, keeping all things crucial in an easily accessible "file," while closing those that offered no real benefit. And, since many childhood memories were emotion-based, they might not register as critical.

Hannah remembered that this explanation had bothered her; did this somehow make her less human? Was she an emotionless robot?

Of course not, Dr. Armistead had assured her. She undoubtedly had strong emotions, no different than any other teenage girl (Hannah thought of her breakup with Gap as Exhibit A), but her brain chose to prioritize when it came to filing.

"Your incredible artistic skills are proof that you have plenty of emotion bubbling up in there," Dr. Armistead had said. "It takes a lot of love to create the work you do on canvas, not to mention a few other emotions as well. Your brain simply chooses to compartmentalize a bit more than the average person; orderly and logical in most cases, but with an emotional outlet through your paintbrush.

"Think of it this way," the doctor continued. "Memories often condition us. They're not too different from the rings inside a tree trunk. Layer upon layer build up over time, all radiating outward from a beginning deep in the past. They help us to grow, in some respects, but they also form a history that we can examine and trace. Major events might leave a more indelible ring, while lesser events blend into the background." She'd finished with a soft, easy laugh. "You're just fine, Hannah, believe me. Besides, who needs to remember their third birthday party anyway? Lots of scary relatives, loud noises, and maybe a bladder accident."

While the doctor's analysis seemed reasonable to her, there were times when Hannah envied others and their astounding memories. There were other times, however, when she wished she could forget completely. Dr. Armistead had certainly been right about one thing: there were emotions—some of them strong and vivid—woven throughout her subconscious.

She had the Rec Room to herself and had dialed up scenes from her home state of Alaska. They flashed in a slide show against one of the walls, staggering images of beauty and majesty. Snow-capped peaks, followed by rich green forests, bears on guard for salmon, massive chunks of glaciers slicing into the sea. The link with home had undoubtedly brought on her melancholy thoughts, driving her to the edge of tears before she choked them back. She would not let her emotions push her that far.

The door opened, and she saw a figure enter through her peripheral vision. She kept her gaze steady on the screen for another full minute before flicking the desk switch and watching her childhood playground fade to black. By that point Merit was perched atop the table, patiently waiting.

"It's gorgeous," he said, nodding towards the screen. "I'm jealous that I never got to see it firsthand. Is it like most things in life, you take it for granted when you see it all the time?"

"I don't know how anyone could take that for granted," she said. "I suppose if I'd had a few more years it might have lost some of that special feel, but probably not." She pulled out a chair and sat facing him. "You wanted to talk?"

"Nothing major, but I told you we'd have strategy sessions from time to time. And this is one of those times."

She didn't speak, so he hopped off the table and began to pace. "First, let me acknowledge that one of the reasons I felt you'd be a great candidate for Council Leader was your grasp of the science on this trip. That's a given. So please don't misunderstand what I'm about to say. I have it on pretty good authority that you've been doing some work on the radiation issue that the ship is facing."

"And how would you know that?" Hannah said.

"Because you were doing the work right out in the open, in the Dining Hall, and people saw you. People talk, Hannah. Word travels."

"Especially in your circles, I see," she said.

He never broke stride, continuing to pace around the table, but a smile spread across his face. "Yes, I know, you've made it clear you don't like me, but we're past that, right? Let's just stay on subject, shall we? The point is, you're doing what you do best, which is solve problems. Again, that's why you're a natural to replace Triana. But I'd like to suggest something if I may."

"Yes?"

"When you solve this radiation problem—and I have no doubt that you'll be the one to figure it out—it would not be a good idea to take it to the Council."

Hannah blinked a few times, watching him take his slow, measured steps. "What are you talking about? If I don't report it to the Council, just who would I tell? What good does it do to figure it out and not use the information?"

"Of course we would use the information. But the last thing

you want to do is tell the Council. If you do that, then Gap gathers the crew together, or makes a ship-wide announcement through e-mail, and although he might mention you somewhere in the fine print, just who do you think would get the credit?"

He had circled the table a few times. As he came around again, Hannah held out her arm and stopped him. "Would you quit with the pacing? It makes me nervous." She got up and leaned against the table. "What are you suggesting I do?"

Merit grinned at her again and pushed a long stray hair behind his ear. "I'm suggesting that you wait until one of the forum sessions of the campaign and break the news to the entire crew. Use the platform, Hannah; that's what it's all about."

It took a few moments, but finally an incredulous smile broke across her face. "You are unbelievable. The ship could be in real danger, and you want me to sit on information that might save us, all for the sake of a few votes?"

Merit sat beside her on the table. "You're not going to have to sit on it, at least not for long. I have every confidence that you'll crack this problem pretty quickly, and there are two forums within the next few days. Chances are you'll have the information just hours before you speak. Besides . . ." He placed a hand on her shoulder. "You'll need a little time to confirm your findings, right? Don't want to rush into an emergency Council meeting without being completely prepared."

Hannah felt her stomach tighten. She suddenly knew that she had crawled into something that was against her nature; it not only didn't feel right, it felt . . . slimy. And yet, as much as it pained her to admit it, there was a measure of truth to what Merit was saying. Whoever delivered the information to the crew was bound to get the credit by default, whether they had done the work or not. Had it been Triana in charge and divulging the solution to the crew, Hannah would have no problem. But Gap?

"So," Merit said, "do we understand each other? Keep doing the work, and find that solution. But stop doing the work in public, and by all means don't report anything to anyone until we're ready."

Hannah turned her head to look at him with dead eyes. *"We're?"*

The smile on his face vanished, and he stood up. "I hope I wasn't wrong about you, Hannah. I hope you have the guts to do this, and to do it right. If you're going to constantly take your eye off the prize and worry about our collaboration, then you're going to fail. Stay focused."

He turned and walked towards the door, stopping short and turning back to face her. "Think you can handle that?"

A moment later he was gone. Hannah leaned back on the table and closed her eyes.

Merit's intentions were obvious to her; he held a festering grudge against Gap and was delighted to use Hannah as a pawn in his scheme for revenge. If he couldn't defeat Gap himself, the next best thing would be to mastermind a campaign to defeat his foe. What better choice, he must have concluded, than Hannah, Gap's one-time girlfriend?

Her own intentions were much more complicated. She couldn't deny that the break from Gap still carried its bitter sting, one that had refused to fade. Give it time, she'd told herself over and over again; give it time. And yet time seemed only to magnify the sense of loss, and the feeling of rejection, to the point where her routines had been shaken, a sure sign that she was still far from recovered.

She had allowed herself to be talked into running against Gap for the position of Council Leader, but it had nothing to do with vengeance. Although the shock of Gap's sudden rebuff had opened old wounds and hurt her deeply, she found that she was unable to summon a desire to strike back at him.

No. What Hannah wanted—what she *needed*—was to prove to Gap that she had been—and still *was*—worth more than he had ever appreciated. She was more than her quiet demeanor suggested. She was . . . valuable. What better acknowledgment of that fact than a successful run to the top spot on *Galahad*'s Council?

It was, she decided, the most direct evidence of the change that she'd experienced after the painful split from Gap. In the past she'd always focused every bit of energy on her art, her scientific curiosity, her love of space and its bizarre puzzles. Now she was able to divert at least a portion of that energy into her self-esteem. Where in the past she'd accepted a role in the shadows, this new awareness pushed and prodded her, demanding she be recognized for her contributions. If not by the whole crew, she admitted, then at least by the one person who had taken her for granted.

It meant forming a distasteful alliance with a person like Merit Simms, but that was a trade-off that she judged acceptable. Merit had his reasons, she had her own; it wasn't important that they intersect. In the meantime, he could help her maneuver her way through an election, where otherwise she might be lost.

She only hoped that she didn't lose herself along the way.

11

She reminds me of Halloween," Gap said to Channy. They were the first to arrive for the Council meeting and, in what had almost become an unspoken tradition, sat outside the Conference Room against the gently curved walls. Recently they never entered the room until all of the members were present in the corridor; it was as if they had a pre-meeting before the actual meeting.

Channy rubbed the belly of Iris, who lay sprawled against the wall. The cat closed her eyes and seemed to soak in the attention.

"But she's black and orange, not solid black," Channy said. "I thought it was black cats that people were afraid of."

"I think of Halloween when I see black and orange," Gap said. "Something about those colors. The decorations, the candy. She's more of a Halloween cat than a black cat would be, if you ask me."

Channy put on her best baby-voice while rubbing Iris again. "But she's not scary at all. Are you? No, you're not."

Gap smiled at the sound. It was good to see Channy acting like herself again after the rough stretch she had been through in the past few weeks. He thought about addressing that, then quickly decided against it; best to simply let her be and not draw attention to it.

Lita strolled into view and immediately slid to the floor beside Channy and began to scratch Iris under her chin. "Greetings, fellow galactic travelers."

Channy giggled. "I like that: galactic travelers. You know, as funny as it sounds, sometimes I get so caught up in the day-to-day routine—you know, eat breakfast, work out, file reports, eat lunch, lead afternoon dance class, so on and so on—that I almost forget that I'm inside a spacecraft. I mean, at first it was on my mind all the time. But now, after a year, if I don't look out through the domes or one of the windows, I just go about my day."

"No, I get it," Lita said. "I'm the same way. Or, if there's some sort of emergency, then it suddenly reminds me, 'Hey, I'm billions of miles from home.'" She looked across the hallway at Gap. "Like this latest fight. That makes two in the last couple of days. Definitely reminders that we're on our own. And, I might add, we're not doing too well keeping it together."

Gap let out a long breath. "I know, I know. We're going to talk about that. Plus a few other things, including the radiation issue, and the Council itself."

"The election?"

"That, and some other issues that I think we need to discuss."

Lita raised an eyebrow. "Sounds interesting. Has one of *us* been bad, too?"

Gap laughed. "Lita, the day you are bad I will jump out an airlock without a helmet."

They made small talk for another minute or two before Bon

walked up. He gave a sullen nod to their greetings, the damage in the dome likely pushing him even farther into a funk. Then as a group they collected their things and walked into the Conference Room. Channy placed Iris onto one of the empty seats, and the cat wasted no time in getting comfortable and beginning to groom. The Council members sat down around the table.

For the first ten minutes they covered the basics, mostly department reports and crew requests. By now they were comfortable with the regimen, and wasted little time ticking items off the list. Gap noted that this time, however, there weren't the usual snarky comments and jokes. Even Roc, normally quick to inject sarcasm at any moment, was reserved.

"If there's nothing else we need to cover," Gap said, "let's talk about our latest bit of drama." He looked at Lita. "How's Karl?"

"Bandaged up and recovering. But he's lucky; the torn shell missed his femoral artery by about an inch."

"So what started all of that?" Channy said.

Lita looked back at Gap for an answer. He shook his head. "Something minor. It should never have escalated like it did. Apparently Karl was sent up from the kitchen area to inquire about a missing delivery from that afternoon. He ended up asking Liam, who mouthed off to him. From what I hear they've argued before. This time words were exchanged, a few insults, and then . . . well, then you know what happened."

"It's ridiculous and immature," Lita said. She turned to Bon. "How bad is the damage?"

The Swede growled his answer. "The irrigation pump is wrecked. It will take a few days to get it back in working order. And, since it was one of the master units, we need to divert activity from other stations. Some of those automatically shut down when the master unit failed. Two of them are not booting back up."

"Will we lose crops?" Gap said.

"I don't lose crops," Bon said.

Gap let out a long breath. "Yes, under normal circumstances. Realistically, will we lose crops?"

Bon tapped one finger on the table and seemed to chew on his answer. "If we do, it won't be for long."

For the first time since the launch, *Galahad*'s Council considered their precarious reliance on the Farm's production. It had seemed a given that the artificial light would always shine upon a flourishing bounty of food. The threat of loss—any loss, no matter how minor—to that production sent a noticeable chill through the room.

Gap thought, "We take too many things for granted."

He gave a nod to Bon. "Okay. Let Engineering know if you need any special help with the repairs. We've had our share of experience with those particular units. And, for the record, I'll be talking with both Liam and Karl. I've had enough of these fights, and I won't tolerate any more reckless, irresponsible behavior. When we get to the point that it's affecting our very survival . . ." He let the thought die.

"If I have to call a special crew meeting, I will," he said, looking around the table. "For now, let's move on to our other issues. We've officially had four 'events' with the radiation shield. The first lasted less than a second; the next time it was about a second and a half. Then it happened twice overnight, again for barely a second. All of the diagnostics that we've run so far tell us that the failures aren't coming from the unit itself. At least not that we can see."

Gap was surprised when Bon immediately spoke up. "Have you considered replacing the unit with the backup? If the replacement doesn't fail, you would have time to find the problem in the original."

"We not only considered it, but that's exactly what Ruben is doing this morning. I won't lie, I think it's a waste of time. But it's the only way to confirm that the problem is not coming from inside the ship, but outside."

Lita scowled. "Outside. So that means our shields aren't equipped to handle the radiation beyond our solar system?"

"No, that's not necessarily true," Gap said. "Roc and I had a talk about that early this morning. Roc, would you care to fill them in?"

"It's possible that it's not radiation at all," the computer said. "Yes, the unit being affected is designed to shove those nasty radiation particles out of our way, so that I don't fry my circuits and you don't grow a second nose. But that doesn't mean it has to be radiation causing the problem.

"Instead, it could be a variety of problems individually, or a series of them, that somehow don't play well with our shield. We've had more than a few encounters recently with what we have labeled dark energy. That's one possibility."

Channy sighed. "Those wormholes. That's it, isn't it? The wormholes have somehow attacked us."

"We're not jumping to any conclusions," Gap said. "We're considering all of the options."

"But the way those things rattled the ship," Channy said. "It only makes sense—"

"Like I said, we're not jumping to conclusions."

"Actually," Roc said, "the wormholes are a consideration. It has been suggested that energy, in the form of radiation, might have leaked out before they pinged out of existence. However, the arguments against that scenario are also strong. Namely, if they did indeed burp out some nasty particles, we would have felt them before this. And, additionally, it wouldn't explain the random nature of the failures.

"That leaves us with interstellar space itself," the computer continued. "Possibly another force altogether, or perhaps something in the nature of deep space that we could never detect from Earth."

"The nature of space?" Channy said.

"The fabric of space is another way to put it," Roc said. "The manner in which the particles and molecules react and interact. Science does its best to explain how they work together, but we don't even know what we don't know, to put it in a quaint but confusing form. And remember: every mile that we scoot along out here is another mile farther into the unknown."

There was quiet around the table as the Council absorbed this. Finally Lita looked at Gap and said, "And the strange flash of light. Is that part of this somehow?"

"That," Gap said, "is yet another mystery. Like we don't have enough already, right? But since there is practically nothing to go on—no residue, no trace of any kind—we don't have much to investigate. It happened, and Roc says it contained strange particles mixed in with the light's photons. If you're asking if it could be somehow connected to the wormholes . . . I have no idea."

Channy looked worried. "So many unknowns. What do we do?"

Gap laced his fingers together on the table. If he was elected Council Leader, that would be a question he'd need to get used to.

"As far as the shields are concerned, the first step is identifying the problem," he said. "We can't come up with a solution until we know what's causing the failures in the first place. Since we're almost positive that it's external, we can focus on that.

"Next we pour every piece of data we can find into the mix and see if there's a pattern. Then we isolate where it's coming from and build a defense system to overcome it."

"You make it sound easy," Channy said.

"It's not going to be easy," Gap said. "But tell me one thing that has been easy on this mission so far."

This was greeted with grim nods.

"And one last thing," Gap added. "The cumulative damage from the failures is mounting. Now that it's happened four times, Roc has run some fairly precise calculations. I'll let him break that good news to you."

"Why do I have to be the bad guy?" the computer said. "All right, to be blunt, whatever is knocking the shields offline is also shaving away their effectiveness. Meaning that with each blow we lose some of our ability to block the radiation. And it's exponential. So, given that cheery bit of information, I can tell you that if the failures continue to occur at this rate, we have about five weeks before we'll be lying on the surface of the sun. Metaphorically speaking, of course."

A deathly silence fell over the room for a few moments before Roc added, "But don't worry, you won't get sunburned, because all of your skin will have rotted away a good day or two before that."

Channy put her hands against the sides of her head and groaned. "Gap, why don't you break the news next time?"

Lita squinted, deep in thought. "So we not only have to figure this problem out, we've got to do it fast. Figure out what's causing it, and what to do about it."

"Correct," Gap said. "The team in Engineering is working overtime, and I'm confident that we'll find a solution long before it turns critical."

Channy and Lita nodded slowly; Bon merely stared down the table at Gap.

When there were no further questions about the radiation problem, they spent a few minutes revisiting the procedures which would govern the election of a new Council Leader. Gap felt a little awkward overseeing this discussion, but did his best to shepherd the meeting through the details. There would be two forums held where the candidates could address the ship's priorities, as well as their own personal qualifications. Questions would follow from the crew.

"Okay," Gap said. "Let's plan on the first forum tomorrow evening, then we'll plug in the final one for Friday evening. The election itself will take place Saturday. Any questions or comments?"

There were none. That meant it was time for him to address the issue which he dreaded the most.

"The last item I want to talk about has to do with the Cassini. In particular, I think it's important for the Council to be fully in the loop about our contact with them."

He sat back and did his best to adopt a relaxed look. He was careful to maintain balanced eye contact with the other three Council members, including Bon. The last thing he wanted was for Bon to think he was intimidated.

"As you know, our only link to the Cassini has been through a connection that none of us really understand. Somehow Bon's brain waves are suited for him to communicate with them, and we've been able to use that connection to help us through a tough stretch. Since we don't really know how the link works, I think Lita would agree that we're also not sure what effects it might be having on Bon, both short-term and long-term."

Lita merely nodded, but it was evident that she was confused as to why they were having this discussion now. Bon sat still, his icy stare never wavering. Gap plowed on.

"Triana was concerned about the danger this connection might have, and so she held on to the translator. In a way, she acted like a guardian. As you know, she would bring it to Bon for the link, and she stayed right by his side to make sure everything turned out okay. Then, she took the translator back to her room."

"I'm sorry," Channy said, "I'm not trying to be difficult, but what does this have to do with anything right now?"

Gap stole another glance at the end of the table, and his eyes locked up with Bon's. For a moment he thought he saw a flicker of anger, but if so, it passed quickly, and Bon was once again stone-faced.

"I bring this up," Gap said, turning to Channy, "because before she left on that pod, Triana left the translator with Bon."

Both Channy and Lita turned to look at Bon, who responded by slowly lifting his cup of water for a drink, never taking his eyes off Gap.

"But you haven't used it, I hope?" Lita said. "At least not by yourself."

"I have," Bon said.

Lita's shoulders sagged. "Oh, Bon. What are you doing?" When he didn't answer, she added, "How many times have you made contact?"

He finally turned his gaze towards Lita. "That's not important. There's no problem, so you shouldn't be concerned."

"Shouldn't be concerned? Your health is my responsibility on this ship, Bon. If Triana was convinced that you should never make that connection alone, what makes you think it's okay now?"

Channy broke in before he could answer. "And why did Triana leave that thing with you in the first place? What did she tell you?"

"She didn't tell me anything. She left it on my desk."

"Well, I think you need to turn it in to the Council," Channy said.

Lita looked puzzled. "Wait a minute. We're out of the Kuiper Belt; why would you connect with the Cassini now?"

Bon shifted his gaze from Lita to Gap, then back again. "Personal reasons."

Lita shook her head. "I don't believe this." She said to Gap, "He can't keep this thing. It's pretty clear that his judgment is already screwed up."

"I agree," Gap said. "That's why I brought it to the attention of the Council. Bon, I think it's obvious how we feel about this. Are you going to make us go through the motions of a formal vote, or will you just hand over the translator?"

Bon took another drink of water. When he spoke, his voice was low but firm. "As of this meeting, Triana is still officially the Council Leader. And, since she chose to give me the responsibility, I will keep the translator until a new Council Leader is elected in her place. Then, at that time, we will see what the new Leader has to say."

It was a double shot, and Gap knew it; Bon was not only

defying his position as the interim Council Leader, he was calling into question whether Gap would even have the position after the Saturday election. And while he burned inside to fire back, he reached deep inside and summoned every ounce of poise that he could find. In the end, he smiled at Bon.

"I believe that if we were to consult the fine print of our bylaws, Bon, you'd be wrong. But I'm willing to let it go until Saturday."

Lita let out an exasperated sound. "No! This is not some petty power struggle we're talking about. This is a matter of the safety and well-being of a crew member."

Gap nodded once. "That's right. And if it involved the safety of others, I would feel differently. If Bon wanted to Airboard without a helmet I would think he was foolish, but I wouldn't stop him unless he was a menace to others."

"This is *not* the same thing," Lita said. "How can you compare the two?"

Gap slowly sipped his own drink of water, then studied the cup in his hand. "Triana had to know that Bon was going to use the translator. If she didn't have a problem with it, then I can let it slide for a few more days."

Channy held her hands out, palms up. "But we don't know what the Cassini will do! What if something goes wrong? It already has once."

There was silence for a minute. It was obvious to Gap that Bon wasn't going to utter another word; he had won again, for the second day in a row, and he knew it.

"I don't suppose you'll let me know if you connect again," Lita said to Bon. "You're just hardheaded enough to think you don't need any help."

He only stared back at her, prompting another exasperated

sigh from *Galahad's* Health Director. She stood up and pushed back from the table. "I want to go on record as being strongly opposed to this."

"Noted," Gap said. Lita turned and walked out of the room.

Channy sat with a stunned look on her face. "Well . . . I'm opposed to it as well," she said.

Gap smiled at her. "Noted as well. Thank you, Channy." He looked back at Bon. "This meeting is over. Everyone stay in touch with me, because if things turn sour with the radiation shield I want to be able to meet immediately if necessary." He stood and followed Lita's path out the door.

Channy, left alone with Bon, refused to make eye contact with him. "You say it's personal, your business with the Cassini. Well, I wish you'd found some personal feelings before this. It's a little late now, if you ask me."

She rose and quickly walked out. For the next few minutes Bon sat by himself in the Conference Room, sipping his water.

Thinking.

12

He usually played Masego against Roc in the Rec Room, but tonight Gap chose to stay in his room. It had been a brutally long day: his run-in with Bon in the Council meeting; another violent confrontation between crew members, one that could potentially mean the loss of food inventory; not to mention endless tests of the radiation shield in the Engineering Section. He was exhausted physically and mentally, and the idea of a large crowd bubbling around him did not sound appealing. His roommate, Daniil, had picked up on Gap's weariness and politely excused himself to meet up with friends.

Faint sounds of rainfall escaped from the room's speakers. Gap's family had relocated from China to America's northwest corner, so he found the sound comforting. It was a frequent soundtrack choice when he was alone.

The vidscreen displayed the Masego board, but Gap's attention wandered. In twenty-four hours he would address the crew again, only this time it would be an audition. He was torn between knuckling down and preparing for the meeting, or unplugging his whirling mind and finding a distraction. He'd hoped that another fruitless contest against Roc, with a healthy dose of the computer's sarcastic observations, would take his mind off everything that had piled up in the last week.

It didn't.

Slumped in his chair, he tapped at the folded sheet of paper on the desk, flicking it back and forth. A battle raged within him, one side telling him to read the note again, another urging him to lock it away, or even to destroy it. Another tap sent the note spinning.

"Are you going to make a move?" the computer said.

"Just a minute," Gap said. He eyed the paper, prepared to stow it away in a drawer. But instead he watched his hand snake out and grasp the folded page. In a moment it was open, and he once again scanned Triana's handwriting.

Gap, I know that my decision will likely anger you and the other Council members, but in my opinion there was no time for debate, especially one that would more than likely end in a stalemate.

There are too many unknowns for us to make the important decisions we face. The wormholes, the vultures, and, most importantly, the beings that are behind both of these. We have to know what we're dealing with.

I don't want to risk taking the ship through a wormhole until we know more about them, and yet I don't want to wait to find out what might come through from the other side.

I'm going through.

I understand the pressure this will put on the Council, and you especially, and for that I'm sorry. But I hope that at some point, when you're able to step back and look at it from a perspective of time, you'll understand why I did this. As you take on more leadership responsibilities I think it will become much more clear.

As for the other issues that you must deal with, all I can offer is the advice I received from Dr. Zimmer: "Do what is right. Your heart may fight you at times, but you always know what is right."

Good luck. Until I see you again . . . Tree

Gap read the last few lines twice. Triana—and Dr. Zimmer—were right: his heart seemed to fight him, even when he knew what was right. It was so hard.

Before he folded the paper again, he looked at her final words and wondered if he would indeed see her again. For now, he—

"Is this a new tactic?" Roc said, shaking him from his trance. "Stalling? Do you think all of the other duties that I'm working on simultaneously will distract me enough so that you can finally win?"

"Sorry, Roc, I'm just not into Masego tonight. Can't shut off my monkey mind."

"I could play with half my circuits tied behind my motherboard."

"And you'd still whip me. Not before letting me think I had a chance, of course, just to keep me interested."

The computer manufactured an exaggerated sigh. "What's the matter, Bunky? Feeling a bit overwhelmed? Do you need a hug? It would have to be virtual, of course, but you know if I had arms I would, right?"

"No, I'm . . . Well, yes, all right, I'll be honest. I'm feeling a touch overwhelmed right now," Gap said. He casually slipped the folded note back into a desk drawer.

"That's not surprising," Roc said. "I've read a few million articles about this emotion in humans, and the consensus from the experts is that you should quit trying to scale the whole mountain and just concentrate on a single step. Sounds reasonable, and yet impossible."

Gap laughed. "Agreed! Sometimes I have a hard time seeing the next step because it seems like the whole mountain is about to collapse on me. What do the experts have to say about *that?*"

"Well," Roc said, "why don't we humor them and try their technique for a moment? What is one item in your overwhelming stack?"

"Ugh, where to begin? Okay, the radiation shield. If we don't figure that out pronto it's lights out."

"And you have about a dozen people hard at work on that right now," Roc said. "Not to mention the services of my brilliant self. Trust that it will be resolved."

Gap slid off the chair and sprawled across the floor into a position that he found the most relaxing. He laced his fingers behind his head and stared up at the ceiling. "Right. Then there's the latest headache with Bon. I can't figure that guy out; sometimes he's this close to actually being civil, then he throws on the brakes and goes back to being . . . Oh, what's a good word? Insufferable. Yeah, that's it. My mom used that word a lot, and I think it applies to Bon. He can be insufferable."

"He said that he would defer to the Council Leader's wishes, however," Roc said. "Surely you don't think he'll cause any damage before the end of the week, do you?"

Gap thought about this for a moment before answering. "Well, probably not. But this whole Cassini thing is such a wild card. We have no idea what we're really messing with, you know? Bon said that it's personal, so I don't see how that could hurt the ship. At the same time, though, if he damages himself then we lose the one person who's able to speak with the Cassini. Lita's worried about brain damage, and I agree with her."

"Then let's assume for the time being that the ship will survive Bon's connection, at least through this weekend," Roc said. "What else?"

"The election."

"Yes, what about it?"

"What do you mean, 'what about it'? It's kind of a big deal, wouldn't you say?"

"Yes, it's a big deal," Roc said. "But worrying about it is pointless. Prepare, do your best, accept what happens."

"Easy for you to say."

"Do you have any idea what kind of work went into programming me so that I can actually speak? Nothing is easy for me to say. I'm a phenomenon, a true miracle of science."

Gap moved his hands from behind his head and covered his eyes with one arm. Talking with Roc was always an exercise in patience, but he had to admit that the repartee made him feel better.

His mind whirled through the other items in his stack, and, as it had for the past couple of days, arrived at the same place: Hannah. Could he talk to Roc about that?

"Let me ask you something," he said, his voice slightly muffled by the arm across his face. "When we have talks like this, are you bound by some sort of confidentiality agreement? You know, like back home, with psychiatrists and priests? Does this conversation stay here, or will I hear it replayed inside the Dining Hall during lunch someday?"

"Yes, you can talk to me about Hannah and it will remain private between us."

Gap slowly pulled his arm away and sat up on his elbows. "You scare me sometimes."

"You're not as tough to read as you think, Gap. What, did you think we'd have to be hush-hush about a discussion on ion drive power modification? I got news for you, pal, the whole crew is fairly amused that the election of a new Council Leader comes down to two people who were all kissy-face just a few weeks ago."

Lying back again, Gap's gaze returned to the ceiling. "I know, I know. What did they use to call those daytime television shows a long time ago?"

"Soap operas."

"That's it. Well, I know this is like a real-life soap opera, but when you're in the middle of the drama it's no fun. And since when were you programmed to use phrases like 'kissy-face'? Please don't say that again; coming from you it's just too weird."

"So what do you want to talk about? Open up to Brother Roc. It stays right here with us."

Gap thought about it. Despite the fact that his mind was racing out of control, he was at a complete loss as to where to begin. It all seemed so . . . irrational. Embarrassment washed over him, and suddenly he regretted broaching the subject at all.

"Oh, never mind," he said.

"Chicken," Roc said. "Listen, you lie there and contemplate the ceiling tiles, and I'll tell you what I deduce from our history together. It's not the possibility of losing the election that bothers you, and it's not even the fact that you could possibly lose to someone you had a relationship with. It's this little corner of your mind that whispers to you that you're somehow not worthy. Forget whether the crew believes in you or not; your first priority is to believe in yourself. I haven't seen these doubts in yourself until recently, but I'll bet they've always been there. You just covered them up with a big, toothy smile and a bucket full of charm."

"That's a fancy way of saying I'm insecure," Gap said. "I suppose that makes me unfit to lead."

"I don't want to say you sound stupid when you talk like that, but I'm going to anyway," Roc said. "You sound stupid. You must think that everyone else on this ship is blessed with total and complete confidence in themselves, and that no one else has self-doubts. That would be a gross miscalculation. There's not a human being walking these curved corridors who doesn't hear the same whispers you do, just in different flavors. One person has self-doubts about their intelligence, another about their looks, another about their artistic talents, another about their leadership. Are you getting the picture here?"

"I'm getting a verbal spanking, that's what I'm getting."

"You better be glad I don't have those arms after all, because instead of a hug right now I'd be thumping you on the head."

Gap couldn't help but smile. "Did Roy have a violent streak in him, too?"

"Roy had more common sense than just about anyone I know, and he was also just about the smartest computer engineer in history. But I spent thousands of hours talking with him while he fine-tuned my programming, and I could rattle off a handful of his insecurities, too. Here's what made him different from most humans, though: he acknowledged those insecurities, and actually worked at them, rather than use them as an excuse."

Shifting onto one side, Gap propped his head up with one hand. He thought about Roy Orzini, the diminutive man who befriended many of *Galahad's* crew members during their training. Gap and Roy had verbally sparred, and it was only natural for Roc to pick up where Roy left off. If Roy had carried around self-doubts, they certainly never showed.

Well, Gap thought, I guess we all wear masks of some sort, don't we?

"I always thought he might be a bit touchy about his height," he said.

"And there you would be wrong again," the computer said. "*You* might have felt that way if you were his size, but Roy never gave that a bit of worry. In his eyes, physical appearance was the least important of any human attribute. In fact, he felt that it gave him an advantage of sorts, because people often underestimated him purely by sizing him up. I think he felt sorry for people who believed their looks or body type were their most important characteristics. And yet he understood that the vast majority of people live in a very shallow pool. He chose to play in the mental end of the pool, where size didn't matter at all. And, I think you'll agree, the man did quite well for himself."

There was no question about that. Gap felt ashamed for automatically assuming that Roy was burdened by a physical trait that, in reality, meant nothing. Perhaps, he thought, we'd all be much better off if we drifted closer to that mental end of the pool.

"Still wanna talk about Hannah?" Roc said with a touch of humor in his voice.

"No," Gap said. "Maybe another time."

He pushed himself to his feet and stretched. His muscles ached, but not from overuse. In fact, just the opposite, he decided. A good night's sleep would be helpful, along with a good workout to burn off some stress. On top of that, it had been much too long since he'd visited the Airboard track, his favorite diversion. All of that would have to wait, however, until he prepared some notes for the first election forum.

Before he could sit down to compose his thoughts, Roc spoke up again.

"Don't get comfortable. Another shield failure in Engineering."

Gap stopped and immediately twisted around, looking for his shoes. "How long this time?"

"Three seconds, then one and a half."

"*Two* failures?"

"That's correct. Fifteen seconds apart."

Without stopping to put them on, Gap snatched up his shoes and darted for the door. "Let them know I'm on my way," he called out to the computer.

13

Her notes were well organized, with each crisp point intended to highlight a fundamental difference between Gap's leadership style and hers. She had read them aloud, over and over again, for almost two hours, working on her delivery, her tempo, even her smile. And yet, as the clock on her vidscreen clicked over to 10:00 p.m., Hannah felt compelled to delete everything and start over again.

There were no errors in the presentation, and her points were valid; some might even be shared by a few of the crew members who would be judging the candidates' performance in less than twenty-four hours. But there was nothing that would make the crew sit up straight and question the ship's status quo. There was little substance in the presentation, and Hannah knew that in order to shake up the system she would have to offer an alternative that was compelling, that inspired voters to take action. As of now, the knockout punch was missing.

She knew what that punch required: information that would shed light on the potentially deadly radiation problem. At the moment, that was the only issue with the weight to shift the balance of power. Despite her best efforts, the answer eluded her. And that, more than the frustration over a lackluster presentation to the crew, put her on edge. Puzzles were meant to be solved.

On a whim she saved her notes, closed the program, and pulled up the event log from Engineering. In a flash she saw that two additional failures of the radiation shield had occurred in the last hour. An adrenaline rush overtook her, and she stood up and stared at the screen, scanning each line of the notations. For a moment she considered running down to Engineering to immerse herself in what was likely a hectic scene. It was easily the best way to get the information she needed, rather than waiting for a log posting which might take an hour or better.

Two things kept her from moving. One, there was a full complement of Engineering staffers who would be hard at work. She would only be in the way. But more importantly, Gap was sure to be there. Merit's warnings echoed through her mind, telling her to keep her investigation under cover. Gap would know in an instant that she was desperately trying to scoop him on the crisis.

Hannah forced herself to sit back down and monitor the readings. With any luck she'd have full details before midnight and could once again delve into the mystery with all new data. In the meantime, she had to make the most of what was available—which wasn't much.

She was growing tired and frustrated, and, to top it off, her bruised leg still ached. She looked at it, gingerly probing with a finger, frowning, and silently scolding herself again for her clumsy behavior.

In front of Gap, no less.

She stared at the bruise. The ugly discoloration was like an accusing eye, staring back at her, an almost circular patch, dark purple and yellow, with reddish-black tendrils splintering away in several directions. A nasty reminder, she realized, of a meeting that never should have taken place. Evidence of a decision that might turn out to be the worst she'd ever made. Evidence . . .

Wait a minute, she though. That's it. Evidence.

A new idea began to vie for her attention. Vague to begin with, it slowly took shape and gathered momentum. By eleven o'clock she had scratched out a series of notes and questions, plugging in holes here, beginning completely new threads there.

By midnight it consumed her. And with it came a new feeling of confidence.

F rustration tore through Gap as he walked out of Engineering. Following the two malfunctions of the radiation shield the night before, he'd spent almost three hours with his staff, going over the data again and again. The only good news—if it could be considered as such—was that the latest glitches essentially confirmed that the problem was not in their equipment. Both the original radiation shield and its replacement counterpart had gone down, which could only mean that the cause came from outside the ship. That freed the crew from any more diagnostic checks.

Gap had stumbled back to his room well after midnight, then turned around and reported back to his post around 7:00 a.m. Now, after almost five hours of investigation and experimentation, he felt exhausted.

And hungry. It dawned on him that he'd not eaten since a quick dinner the night before; it helped explain not only the weariness that weighed on him, but also his mood, which was decidedly foul. When he'd snapped at Julya for no reason, he knew it was time to walk away and eat something. No doubt his blood sugar level had cratered, dragging his attitude with it.

But there was another factor involved. Just before falling into bed the night before, he'd sent a quick e-mail to the other Council members, updating them on the latest development. He'd also requested a quick response with their department reports, in lieu of a Council meeting. There were responses from Channy and Lita when he awoke, but nothing from Bon. And now, as he left Engineering, the report was still missing.

That, as much as the baffling radiation problem, merely added to the frustration he carried. In fact, his irritation with Bon had officially reached the breaking point. Stepping into the lift, he decided to put his grumbling stomach on hold for a bit longer and do something about it.

The doors opened and he stepped into the humid air of the domes. It was lunchtime on *Galahad*, so activity at the Farms was subdued. Three crew members waved as Gap trudged down the path, but they were the only people he saw.

Bon would certainly not be anywhere near the Dining Hall, not during the height of the lunch rush. He would likely be found either in his office or in the fields, working alone on a project while his team members were taking their noon break. Although he bristled at Bon's contentious manner, Gap could never fault his work ethic.

The office was empty. For a split second Gap considered scouring Bon's desk drawers in search of the translator, but discarded the idea. That was not how he wanted to lead. He turned and walked out, then stood with his hands on his hips, scanning the fields as far as he could see. Bon was somewhere out there, but a search could take an hour or more. And Gap was convinced that if he called out as he walked, Bon wouldn't answer, even if he heard.

His stomach growled again, but Gap's irritation overrode his hunger. He set off down the path in a random direction.

After fifteen minutes he chanced upon two other crew members making their way towards the lift, but other than that the dome seemed deserted. He wandered off the path from time to time, pushed thick vegetation aside, then made his way back to the path. Soon he began a routine of stopping every hundred feet or so and listening. If there was a benefit to searching while the majority of the crew was on break, it was that any sound would carry.

The tactic paid off. He just happened to look down at one point and discovered a faint trail that splintered off the main path. Gap knelt down and noticed shoe impressions in the soft soil. Intrigued, he struck out down the trail, and a minute later heard the muffled sounds.

He held his breath, which was coming in gasps, in order to pinpoint the direction. When it came again, he was sure that it was a voice, crying out in pain, drifting through the lush fields. Scrambling ahead, he pushed aside an overhang of thick leaves and saw Bon.

He was kneeling in a small clearing, his head back, his eyes closed, and a look of intense pain etched across his face. Even from a distance of fifteen feet, it was obvious that he was shaking uncontrollably. With a downward glance, Gap saw the telltale dull red glow of the translator seeping from between Bon's fingers.

Although his first instinct was to rush into the clearing, Gap held himself back. It was Bon's voice that had led him here in the first place; now he wanted to hear what was being exchanged with the Cassini. What was so personal that Bon couldn't—or wouldn't—tell the Council? Gap crept a few feet closer and got down on one knee.

He watched a shudder ripple across Bon, shaking him, forcing his head back even farther. But to Gap it seemed that Bon was fighting whatever forces racked him, stubbornly pushing back against the might of the alien power. It occurred to Gap that, of all the crew members who could have been genetically wired to accommodate the Cassini's peculiar form of communication, perhaps they were lucky that it was Bon. The surly Swede was not one to get pushed around, and that was exactly the kind of representative that the crew of *Galahad* needed.

A small cry broke from Bon's mouth, followed by another spasm. Gap could only imagine what kind of agony he was feeling. What was so important to Bon that he would put himself through this?

"No . . ." Bon said through clenched teeth. "No . . ." His head turned violently to one side, and Gap saw that he was dripping with sweat. His breathing seemed an exercise in torture, and for a second Gap thought that he might collapse. But again he appeared to fight the forces that swept through him. His eyes flickered open briefly, emitting a ghostly orange glow, and his voice seemed to struggle through layers of mud.

"Where . . ."

Gap strained to hear, but the rest was unintelligible. He had the feeling that Bon would be able to detect his presence if he got too close, but he had to know what was being communicated. Slipping quietly to his right, he shifted to within six feet, directly behind Bon, and leaned in.

"Where . . . is . . . she?"

Gap stifled a gasp. Bon had furiously defended his right to a freelance session with the Cassini, and it was all about finding Triana? Why, Gap wondered, wouldn't he want to discuss that with the Council? Why would a search for the Council Leader be something Bon deemed so inappropriate that he wouldn't want to enlist their support? What made this personal?

Could it have something to do with the complicated relationship that Bon and Triana shared? Of all the ship's crew members, Gap alone had firsthand knowledge of that relationship, slim as the evidence might be. He had carried a visual reminder—an embrace—for months, and it still haunted him.

"How . . . do . . . I . . ." Bon never finished the sentence. He cried out again, as if the Cassini were lashing out, punishing him for daring to challenge their control. Before Gap could react, Bon crumpled forward onto the soil. He struck the ground face-first, his hands at his sides. His grip on the translator relaxed, and it rolled a foot away, the glow fading from its vents.

Still on his knees, Gap covered the distance between them in a flash. He turned Bon's face to the side and did his best to wipe away the dirt. Blood began to pool in the Swede's mouth, and his eyes had rolled up. Gap stood and looked back the way he had come, considering his options to get help. But he knew that the domes would likely still be deserted, with a bare-bones crew covering the break. It might take several minutes to backtrack and call for help, and even longer to get Lita or other medical personnel up here.

Gap knelt down and lifted one of Bon's arms. He slowly rose to his feet, lifting the deadweight with him, until he had Bon in a standing position. Then, using his gymnastics training and his formidable strength, he hefted Bon over his shoulder. In seconds he was hustling back along the path, hurrying to get to the lift and down to Sick House.

In the trampled soil of the clearing, artificial sunlight glinted off the spiked, metallic ball.

14

A small knot of crew members huddled together in the outer offices of Sick House, talking in hushed voices. Every few minutes one would peek into the hospital ward, curious about the proceedings, but they all knew to stay out until summoned.

After finishing the most difficult part of the procedure, Lita stepped back and addressed Manu. "Can you get started on the cast? I'm going to update his friends so they can get out of here for now. I'll be right back to help."

She stepped out into the office and looked around at the five faces that stared back at her, all draped with concern. She greeted them with a smile.

"Yes," she said, "it's definitely broken. In two places, to be exact. I guess when Rico does it, he does it big."

This brought a nervous chuckle from the group. One of the girls, Vonya, said to Lita, "But he's okay, right?"

"Oh, sure. He'll be a celebrity of sorts when he walks out of here with that cast. I guess you guys can be the first to sign it."

Lita's casual and confident tone seemed to reassure them. They exchanged relieved glances.

"By the way," Lita said, "I'll need to file a full report. So let me get this straight: Rico was at the Airboard track, but he *wasn't* riding? Micah, you said something about the bleachers, is that right?"

"Uh, yeah. He was up in the stands with some of us, just watching and . . . well, heckling, I guess you could say. Rico's the best Airboarder, you know? But he has more fun than anyone in the stands, too. Anyway, it was almost his turn, so he started to walk down the steps, and when he went to put his helmet on, I guess he misjudged one of the steps, and . . . well, here we are."

Lita shook her head. "Hmm. Maybe he won't be a celebrity after all. If he'd busted his arm on the track it would be one thing. But tripping on the bleachers?"

"Oh, he's still a celebrity on this ship," Vonya said. "No one will ever break his record on the track."

"Don't let Gap hear you say—"

Lita was interrupted by the whoosh of the door. Gap came flying into the room with a body slung over his shoulders. He made quick eye contact with Lita and, without hesitating, bolted for the hospital ward. As he went past, Lita saw that it was Bon who hung limply, with small spatters of blood on his face and Gap's shirt. She told the assembled group that it would be best for them to leave, that Rico would be out in a while, then she turned and ran into the ward.

"Over here," she said to Gap, pointing to a bed against the far wall. Manu, Rico, and two other Sick House workers stared in disbelief. Lita glanced at Manu and said, "Can you finish up without me?"

"No problem," he said.

Gap, covered in sweat, deposited Bon onto the bed. Lita hurried over beside him. "What happened?" she said, bending to look into Bon's face.

Gap was breathing heavily. "He was doing what I was afraid of," he said. "He linked up with the translator. Only this time it knocked him out."

Lita fought back the urge to scold Gap for not taking her advice in the Council meeting, for not insisting that Bon hand over the translator. She bit her tongue, knowing that it served no purpose to bring that up now. The first order of business was to tend to Bon.

His pulse was weak, his breathing shallow. Lita checked his blood pressure, and when it registered extremely low, she frowned. "He's in shock."

Gap rubbed a hand through his hair. "What about the blood?"

"Looks like he landed on his nose and mouth when he collapsed. That doesn't appear to be anything major, just a bit bloody." She continued to work on the Swede, but said over her shoulder to Gap, "You went with him? Why didn't you stop him?"

"No, I didn't go with him. I was looking for him and found him already linked up, hiding out in the fields." He quickly summarized what had happened, including Bon's tortured question.

" 'Where is she?' " Lita said slowly, staring down at Bon. "So . . . is he trying to find Triana?"

"I would assume so. Anyway, that's all he said before he passed out and bit the ground."

"Fool," Lita muttered under her breath. "I suppose it goes against the medical code to slap an unconscious patient."

"I can look the other way," Gap said.

She gave an exasperated sigh. "Listen, it's probably best if you wait out there. We've got some work to do, and then I'll come talk to you." She threw a quick look at Gap. "You okay?"

"Yeah," he said. "Just mad at this creep for doing this, and mad at myself for being worried about him."

Lita smiled before turning back to Bon. "We'll take care of him. If you want, go get yourself cleaned up and I'll talk to you in a bit."

For the first time Gap noticed that another bed was occupied. "Rico? What happened to him?"

"He's a klutz. I'll tell you about it when I talk to you. Go on, you're in the way."

Fifteen minutes later Bon stirred. His eyelids fluttered, then opened. He struggled to raise a hand to his face to shield against the light that seemed to blind him. Lita watched the realization set in as he discovered that he was—once again—in Sick House. This was the second time the Cassini had put him in one of the ward's beds, and his face displayed immediate irritation.

"What . . . why . . ." was all he managed.

"Is this going to become a habit for you?" Lita said, standing beside him. "Should I just move some of the things from your room up here?"

As his eyes grew accustomed to the light he lowered his arm. A moment later it was raised again, this time to inspect the swell of his lip.

"Yes, you look like you've been in a fight," Lita said. "First a bloodied hand, now this." She pulled his hand down from his face. "Don't play with that, you'll pull out the stitch, and the next one won't be free."

He shifted his jaw back and forth, opening and closing his mouth. It reminded Lita of the Tin Man from *The Wizard of Oz*.

"May I at least . . . get some . . . water?" he croaked to her.

"Right here," she said, holding up a cup. She held it for him while he drank through a straw. "How's your head feel?"

He lay back on the pillow and blinked a few times. "It's fine."

"I doubt it," Lita said. "You understand, of course, that in order for a doctor/patient relationship to work, you'll have to be honest with me."

"How did I get here?"

"You had a guardian angel wander by and whisk you to safety."

"Wander by?" Bon said. "Right. Let me guess. Gap."

"Oh, so now you're gonna act indignant after he rushed you here when you passed out? How nice."

Bon fell silent as Manu came over and conferred with Lita about their other patient.

"Sure, he can go if you're finished," she said to her assistant. She glanced over at Rico. "Hey, nice job on the cast. Between that and the patch job you did on Karl, you're racking up an awful lot of experience this week."

"Thanks," Manu said with a grin. "Piece of cake." He escorted Rico out of the ward.

"Okay," Lita said to Bon. "Get some rest. We're gonna run a few tests on you in about an hour."

"What kind of tests? I don't need any tests."

"Well, Dr. Hartsfield," Lita said, "I'm afraid I disagree with your analysis of the patient." She gave Bon the type of scowl that he usually dished out himself. "You might run the Farms, my friend, but I run this department. I won't question the way you do your job, so please don't question me. Deal?"

Bon responded by turning his head away and closing his eyes. Lita made a few notes on a workpad, then walked out to the office. Gap, however, was nowhere to be found. Manu sat alone at his desk.

"Did Gap go back to his room to clean up?" she said.

Manu shook his head. "He hightailed it out of here. Got a call from Engineering."

"Oh no," Lita said, dropping into the chair across from Manu's desk. "That can't be good. The radiation shield?"

"Yes, it dropped out again. But that's not all. About three minutes before that, there was another flash of light. Just like the first one."

Lita frowned. "Are they connected somehow? Or is it just coincidence that they happened so close together?"

Manu shrugged. "Good question."

"I'll tell you this," Lita said. "If Gap and his crew don't figure something out soon, I'm afraid he's gonna end up in the bed next to Bon, just from exhaustion." She set her workpad on his desk and made another note. "I've got to go check on something. Do me a favor, please; in about an hour prep Bon for a series of cranial scans."

Manu raised his eyebrows. "Will do. Anything in particular we're looking for?"

Lita stood up. "To be honest, I want to make sure he's still Bon."

No," Gap said. "I don't want to hear another person say 'I don't know.' We need answers, and we need them right now." He looked at the faces gathered around him. "Throw out anything, and let's talk about it."

His engineering staff stood mute, exchanging quick glances with each other, then looking down at their feet or over Gap's shoulder.

He rubbed a hand through his hair and let out a long breath. "Okay," he said softly. "First of all, I need to sit down for a minute." He dragged a chair over and dropped into it. For a moment he didn't speak, and rubbed his face with both hands. Finally he said, "I know this sounds dumb, but does anyone have anything to eat in here?"

Julya walked away and came back with an apple. "Sorry, it's all I've got."

"No, it's great. Thank you," he said. He took two large bites, swiped at his face with the back of his hand, then spoke with a mouth full of apple. "I'm not trying to be a jerk, but I wonder if everyone understands how bad this is. Forget about the flash for the moment. We still don't know what it is or where it's coming from. Focus on the radiation issue, that's our primary concern. Eventually we're gonna get to the point where the shield goes out and doesn't come back on. And then we're cooked. Literally."

He took another healthy bite. "Right now there are no bad ideas. Anything is better than nothing. C'mon, think. What have we missed?"

There was a shuffling of feet, and a couple of people cleared their throats. Then Wiles, one of the ship's quietest crew members, raised a hand. Gap, taking another bite of the apple, gave him a weary smile. "Wiles, you don't have to raise your hand. Just tell me what you think. Please."

"Well . . . we replaced the unit, and the new one is dropping out, too. Which makes us think that it's got to be coming from outside the ship."

"Right," Gap said. "So?"

"Maybe it's not," Wiles said. "I mean, maybe the shield itself is okay, but something else on the ship is causing it to drop out. Like something is stealing its power or something."

Gap finished the apple with two more bites. He looked at the core in his hand, his mind working over what Wiles was telling him. "It's something to consider. A long shot, I think, but still, it's an idea. Anyone else?"

Julya said, "I once took a sightseeing trip with my family to see a lava flow. There were a bunch of us, all packed on this big boat, and we rode out to where the lava was pouring into the sea. It was beautiful, but terrifying at the same time."

Gap nodded. "Okay. What's the connection here?"

Julya seemed to chew on her thoughts for a moment. "One of the things I remember was the way the surf smacked into the boat. There was so much turbulence under the water, from the lava flow. We'd go for a while with just gentle waves, and then, without any warning, we'd be tossed into the air by some heavy swell. There was nothing leading up to the big ones, no pattern. Smooth one moment, then a shove."

"So you're saying . . . space waves?" Gap said.

"Exactly. We've known for a long time that the solar wind stretches to the edge of our planetary system, out past the Kuiper Belt. Then it smacks head-on into the radiation that the galaxy itself puts out."

Ruben Chavez looked from Julya to Gap. "That's right," he said. "I remember studying that. It's called the termination shock; it's like . . . well, it's like a film surrounding the solar system." He turned back to Julya. "But we passed that point already."

Gap sat forward. His hunger somewhat satisfied by the apple, he was better able to concentrate. "Roc," he called out. "What about this termination shock?"

"Ruben's correct," said the computer. "We have passed the point where the solar winds collide with the incoming galactic radiation. However . . . and aren't you happy to know that there's a 'however'? Doesn't it give you hope?"

"I don't know," Gap said. "Let me hear the 'however.'"

"However, farther out, beyond this sinister-sounding termination shock, we zip through an area called the heliopause. By the way, I didn't make up these scientific terms; they're words that were coined by very lonely people in a lab late at night."

"What's the heliopause?"

"It's the point where the outgoing radiation and incoming radiation are essentially balanced. A few of those lonely folks dreamed up another concept that I like a whole lot more. Bubbles."

"Bubbles?" Gap said. He rubbed his forehead. "Please, explain the bubbles."

The computer seemed to take delight in the discussion. "See, aren't you intrigued already? These interstellar winds that are blowing into our solar system get pushed around it by the outgoing solar wind, like a river rushing around rocks. So some very brilliant people suggested that it forms bubbles as they pass."

Gap looked at Ruben and Julya. "So you're saying that we might be colliding with interstellar bubbles?"

Julya looked at Ruben, then back to Gap. "Yeah, I guess so. Just an idea."

"And a pretty good one," Gap said. "So just to get this straight: we cruise through calm space, like your sightseeing boat, until we bump up against one of these bubbles, just like the waves you described."

Nobody said anything as they all digested this.

"See, I told you it was a fun idea," Roc said. "And now, sadly, and with great regret, I must bring you back down."

"What does that mean?" Gap said.

"Those brilliant scientists, the ones who came up with the space bubble idea? They were pretty sure that, if it happened, it happened at the termination shock, not the heliopause."

"And we've already passed that point."

"See, you're depressed again," the computer said.

Gap stood up and paced the room for a moment. It seemed that every time they inched ahead, they were shoved right back again. Julya's suggestion seemed reasonable to him, and yet Roc had—he winced at the pun—burst their bubble. Wiles's idea about the energy drain from inside the ship was a possibility, but somehow it didn't feel right.

Which put them right back where they were. Gap kept pacing, aware that his team members' eyes were on him. Stay positive, he told himself.

He stopped next to the chair. "Okay, this is what we need," he said. "Ideas. Suggestions. Theories. They at least give us something to work with. And one idea might lead us towards something that we never would have considered. I don't want to discard any of these suggestions right now; let's kick them around a bit. Maybe it is something inside the ship that's affecting the shield. And maybe these bubbles happen farther out than we think. Maybe the lightning that we're seeing has something to do with it all. Keep plugging away, and let's work it out."

The team broke up and moved back to their work spaces. Gap stayed another five minutes, then headed for the Dining Hall.

The first election forum was seven hours away.

15

The music blasting out of the speakers in her room was unlike her usual selections, and the volume was much higher than her normal comfort zone. But Lita bounced lightly to the beat, adjusting her hair in the vanity mirror, turning her head from side to side in order to see how it was coming together. For a moment the sound diminished so the tone from her door could bleed through. She opened the door to find Channy standing there with an incredulous look on her face.

"Whoa! Got your own concert going on in here?"

Lita laughed. "Kinda feels that way, doesn't it?" she yelled over the music. She moved across the room to her desk and lowered the volume to a level where they could talk. Turning back to her mirror she added, "I think I needed an energy boost or something. It's been crazy this week, between the interviews, then the fights, then Bon."

Channy plopped onto Lita's bed, sitting on one foot and letting the other dangle towards the floor. "You must be drained."

"I am. But I don't want to think about it anymore. Tonight

it's loud music, a nice dinner with my friend Channy, and hopefully a full eight hours of sleep. That's what I'm prescribing for myself."

"Hooray!" Channy said, pumping a fist in the air. Then she smiled at Lita's reflection in the mirror. "This isn't even music you normally listen to. It's usually that stuff your mom used to like."

"I'm telling you, tonight I'm cutting loose. I might even start a food fight during dinner."

"You didn't inhale nitrous oxide or anything, did you?" Channy asked, wrinkling her brow.

Lita laughed again and finished adjusting the customary red ribbon in her hair. Then, after examining how it looked, she suddenly pulled the ribbon out and tossed it on the counter. After fumbling through a drawer, she leaned forward and tied a shiny blue ribbon into her hair.

"Okay," Channy said. "I officially don't know who you are tonight. But that's okay, I think I might like this version of Lita. Without the food fight, of course."

"Let's go," Lita said. "I need nourishment, right now."

She turned off the music and together they strolled down to the lift.

"I don't want to upset your mood," Channy said, "but I need to ask you something about our resident grump."

"You won't upset my mood," Lita said. "I don't mind talking about Bon."

"Well, I want to know why it's impossible for him to show any kind of emotion about Alexa. If we're supposed to be impressed by his tough-guy act, it isn't working. In fact, I'm furious with him."

Lita looked puzzled. "Wait, I don't understand what you're saying. You're bothered by how *he's* reacting to her death? Why should that matter to you?"

"Because I think it's disrespectful to Alexa, that's why."

"Oh, Channy, that's ridiculous. No two people grieve the same way, or show emotions the same way. Besides, you have no idea what he's feeling on the inside. I'm pretty sure Bon is just as torn up as you are about Alexa; probably more so. But don't expect him to mourn her the way you do, especially in public."

"Lita, I'm not asking him to go around weeping in front of everyone. But you gotta admit, this stone-faced act is wretched. We both know that he cared about her; they spent hours together."

The lift stopped and they exited into a fairly crowded corridor. It was prime time for dinner on *Galahad*, and the Dining Hall would be packed.

Lita lowered her voice a bit as they walked. "I'll give you this much: Alexa and Bon had a unique relationship, built on their very unique . . . well, gifts, I guess you could say. Or talents." She shook her head. "Anyway, you know what I mean. And I'm pretty sure that Alexa was smitten by our Swedish hunk. Whether *he* was smitten is another story."

"So what are you saying?" Channy said.

"I'm saying that I wouldn't be surprised if a lot of what Bon is feeling right now is guilt."

"Guilt?"

Lita shrugged. "Well, yeah. If he knew how Alexa felt, but he didn't exactly feel the same way, he might be feeling a bit guilty that he didn't reciprocate, and now she's gone."

The door to the Dining Hall was open, and, as expected, a

fairly long line had already formed. Channy and Lita picked up trays and took their place.

Now it was Channy's turn to speak softly. She leaned in toward Lita and said, "You might be right. But I still think the least he could do would be to act sad, on some level. It's like he has something to prove, and I hate that."

"You shouldn't worry about that, Channy. Listen, none of us know what goes on in the hearts and minds of others. It's pretty easy to be fooled by someone's attitude or expressions. Deep down inside you have no idea what's churning away. In fact . . ."

They moved a few steps closer to the first food dispenser and answered several friendly greetings from the crew members around them. Then Lita finished her thought.

"In fact, I'd be willing to bet that Bon is really suffering over this, and just doesn't know how to show it. A lot of it could be his background, his family life . . . who knows? Please don't be so hard on him over this. I think he has a lot more heart than you suspect."

Channy snorted. "You forget, I'm the heart expert on this ship."

"But this time I think you have blinders on."

They began to load up their trays and engaged in light conversation with the people around them, before filling some glasses with water and moving over to an empty table.

As they sat down, Channy gave Lita a sly look. "Just for the record, don't think I didn't pick up on that one comment."

"Oh?" Lita said. "What comment is that?"

"The one where you called Bon a hunk."

Lita smiled and wagged a finger. "Don't even start with me on that stuff, my friend. You can't make a case out of the obvious. There's not a girl on this ship who doesn't think Bon is beautiful. I won't play that game with you."

"Oh, all right," Channy said with a chuckle.

They spent the next five minutes talking about the two fights that now had crew members whispering in hushed circles around the ship.

"I hate to say it," Lita said with a sigh, "but I wondered if something like this might happen after two major shocks hit us so quickly. People react to stress so differently, and the tension can cause tempers to not only flare, but explode."

Channy looked thoughtful. "So you think it's just temporary?"

Galahad's Health Director didn't answer at first, but then shook her head. "Unfortunately, violence often only leads to more violence. I'm worried that it might get worse before it gets better. With Triana gone it's almost like the inmates are running the asylum, and they can't see how much worse they're making everything. It gets out of control, you know?"

She suddenly felt uncomfortable with the topic. "But I could be wrong," she said. "Maybe it is temporary. After the election things might settle down a bit."

There was a lull in the conversation. Channy pushed some lettuce around on her plate with a fork and seemed to search for the best way to express what she was thinking. "I never thought I'd feel this way," she said, "but as the days go by I get more angry at Triana. We shouldn't even be worrying right now about an election for Council Leader." She glanced up to see what reaction her comment had caused. "I mean . . . we need real leadership right now with this radiation thing, and instead we're in a big mess. Now with these fights . . ." Her voice trailed away.

Lita kept her gaze on her own plate. "It's easy to say that now. But when Triana left in the pod there wasn't an issue with the shield, and we can't deny that Triana's intentions were honorable." She lowered her voice and added, "I'm not sure I would've had the courage to do it."

Channy looked up at Lita again and, with a trembling voice, said, "She's not coming back, is she? I've been trying to think positive and all that, but . . . but c'mon, she went through a wormhole! I don't care what Roc says, I don't know how anyone could survive that."

"It's not that," Lita said sadly. "I've thought about it a lot over the last couple of days, and I think she actually might have gone through just fine. No, what worries me the most is how she'll find her way back."

Channy pushed her tray aside and leaned on the table. "Oh. I guess I didn't think about that."

Lita nodded. "I would assume that whoever—or whatever—is responsible for the wormhole that swallowed her up could just as easily open up another one. But how will Triana know where we'll be? We're moving faster and faster each day, and eventually we'll start to approach the speed of light. That means we're moving a long, long way every twenty-four hours; just how will she know where to pop out?"

"Great," Channy said. "Now I'm even more depressed. Is there a way we can send out a signal or something?"

"I don't know. Maybe. But I think that's something we need to at least think about. Triana might, or might not, be coming back. But if there's any chance at all, then we need to become a lighthouse for her."

"Maybe you could bring it up during the forum."

Lita shook her head. "No, I'll just wait and mention it to Gap later. The forum is about their ideas, not mine."

Channy looked across the crowded room. "So what's the word on Bon? Is he still in the hospital?"

"I just sent him back to his room about an hour ago. He won't be at the forum. I'm sure he'll watch it on his vidscreen."

Channy sniffed. "I doubt it. I don't think he cares one way or the other."

"You know," Lita said, "at some point you have to get over this irritation with him. You're both Council members, and you have to work together."

"If you say so," Channy said, then let out a sigh. "Let's talk about something else."

Lita smiled at her and held out a strawberry. "Here, nobody can be blue when they eat one of these. It's delicious."

Channy returned the smile and accepted the gift. "All right, I get the message. Relax, don't overthink things, enjoy what I have, et cetera, et cetera."

Lita winked at her. "You got all of that from a strawberry?"

"You know what you're doing," Channy said. "And thank you. You're right."

"Everything's gonna be fine," Lita said. "Maybe not normal, because we left normal behind a long, long time ago. But it will all work out fine." She stood and picked up her tray. "Before the forum gets started I need to wrap up some things in the Clinic. Oh, and one other thing: I don't think we should sit in the front row tonight."

"Why not? We always sit there during meetings."

"I know," Lita said. "But this is different. A Council spot is on the line, and I don't think we should be there as Council representatives. Tonight we should simply be interested crew members."

"Whatever you think," Channy said. "See you in a bit. And thanks again."

She tossed the remnants of the strawberry onto her plate and wiped her hands. She thought about the upcoming election, which soon had her once again thinking about Triana. Lita had a good point: would any of them have had the courage to do what Triana had done? The Council Leader had essentially sacrificed herself to buy time for the crew of *Galahad*.

Lita had also expressed a concern that Channy had not considered. Would Triana be able to find her way back? Lita had mentioned a lighthouse, which was an apt description. Triana would need a beacon of sorts to zero in on the ship as it streaked out of the solar system and across interstellar space. Did they have the technology to even do that?

And, if they did, would Triana know what to look for?

His instructions from Lita had been clear: go to your room, stay there, and don't even think of reporting to work until the next day. The first part, at least, had been satisfied. Bon sat at the desk in his room while his roommate, Desi, prepared to leave for the forum.

But he had no intention of staying there.

"Do you need anything before I go?" Desi said.

"No, thanks."

"All right. I'll be back after the meeting. Remember, take it easy. Doctor's orders, right?"

Bon gave a slight nod. "Right."

Once he was alone, Bon pushed himself out of the chair, paus-ing momentarily to steady himself as a dizzy spell struck. The forum was scheduled to begin in ten minutes, which meant that the corridors—and the domes—would be empty. Crew members who couldn't attend because of work commitments would be watching on vidscreens around the ship. Even the extra hands working on the damaged irrigation system had a break for this one hour. Bon would be able to slip almost anywhere, unnoticed.

He'd told Lita that his headache was gone, but that had been a lie, crafted to get him out of the hospital as quickly as possible. The pain was centered in the middle of his forehead, a dull ache similar to what he'd experienced during his previous Cassini connections.

But it had never lasted this long.

What concerned him the most, however, was the fact that the link had once again landed him in Sick House. His casual attitude about the alien connection would no longer sway the Council. Because of that, it was imperative that he get back up to Dome 1 immediately. Should he bump into anyone on the way, his story was set: he simply was checking on repairs to the irrigation pump.

He waited another two minutes before slipping into the corri-dor. As expected, it was deserted. Bracing himself against the wall, he lurched along, stopping every few feet to clear his head and regain his balance. Once inside the lift, he leaned back and closed his eyes. When the door opened at the Farms, it took a moment to summon the strength to push himself out.

The humid air energized him somewhat, and, although his head still throbbed, the steps came easier. Passing his office, he trudged along the path towards the clearing. The lights had be-gun their evening cycle and were slowly dimming. Machinery along the route hummed, and an occasional light spray of moisture, carried along by the artificial breezes, struck his face. The cool mist felt good.

For no reason, a sudden image of his father burst into his mind, and with it the familiar mix of emotions. The lifelong farmer from Skane, Sweden, stood against a backdrop of lush, green fields that swayed with a silent wind. His weathered face stared across the months and the miles at Bon as he staggered down the path. His expression made it clear that he was disappointed in his son. No words were necessary; it was a look that Bon had labored under for many years.

Only this time, Bon knew that it had nothing to do with his farming efforts. His father had taught him well, had raised him to respect the land and the bounty that it produced, and had instilled a work ethic that could never be questioned.

No, this look signified something much worse. It said, "You are weak."

Bon's pace slowed for a moment, but then picked up again. "Yes," he said to himself. "I am. I am weak."

He lowered his head and pushed through the final overhang of leaves, into the clearing. The same clearing where he had spent hours talking with Alexa, listening to her pour out her thoughts and her fears. The same clearing that he used as his private sanctuary. The only place he had felt comfortable for the task that called to him.

In the fading light he found the disturbed soil where he'd connected with the Cassini. He dropped to both knees, thankful for the chance to rest and hopefully silence the painful pulse in his head. It should only take a moment, he thought, to find what he was looking for. It had to be right here.

But it wasn't.

He crawled on all fours, fanning out from the spot where he'd collapsed during the link. He brushed his hand through the dirt and craned to look a few feet into the foliage that surrounded him. But it was pointless.

The translator was gone.

Sitting up on his heels, he brushed the dirt from his hands, then pushed a strand of unruly hair from his face. Obviously Gap had pocketed the metallic ball when he'd stumbled upon the clearing and found Bon sprawled unconscious. And of course Gap wouldn't say a word about it, waiting for Bon to bring it up, so he could take back a measure of control.

The light continued to melt away, and the first visible stars began to appear through the panels of the dome. After sitting quietly for another few minutes, Bon finally climbed to his feet and steadied himself. The headache persisted, but now it was magnified by the disgust he felt for himself.

"I am weak," he said again, before turning towards the path and a long, slow walk back to his room.

16

When people sit around and argue I tend to get bored easily. In most cases both sides have already made up their minds, and no amount of screaming and name-calling is going to have an effect. If you want my opinion, many times it's about the screamer trying to convince themselves that they're right, not the other person. The louder the voice, the more insecure they are about their position. Think about it.

But a good old-fashioned debate . . . now THAT'S practical. Sometimes referred to as persuasive speech, two people address a willing audience with the intent of making strong points that will convince the receptive crowd to join their side. It's a valuable exercise, as long as the participants are being honest. By participants I mean both the debaters and the audience. Those arguing their points must present honest information, and those in the crowd must honestly be open to both messages.

Of course—and I'm whispering here—I personally have to admit that a little name-calling, while not productive, is good for a few laughs. Sadly, I don't see either Gap or Hannah stooping to that.

Sigh.

★ ★ ★

Gap felt awkward sitting next to Hannah on the front row of the auditorium, especially since they had exchanged only cordial greetings and then not another word. With one chair separating them, both pretended to be absorbed in their notes, preparing for their moment in the spotlight. He knew that the buzz from the packed house behind them likely included more than a little gossip about the two candidates; the crew, he figured, had to be loving the show.

He found himself using every muscle of his peripheral vision to look at Hannah. Her hair was pulled back and up, a look that he had to admit was stunning. She wore a light blue shirt that, to him, seemed professional, yet warm and approachable. She sat with perfect posture and gave every indication that she was poised and perfectly at ease.

He, on the other hand, felt slumped and nervous. He shifted in his chair, setting his shoulders back and crossing one leg over the other. Tilting his head back, he draped an arm over the back of the chair beside him and accidentally tapped Hannah on the shoulder. "Sorry," he mumbled, moving his hand back to his side.

Lita and Channy were nowhere to be seen, which meant they had chosen to melt into the background. Bon, of course, would not be here, even if he hadn't been sent to his room to recover from the Cassini incident. For the first time since the launch, Gap would be out in front without any visible sign of Council support.

And that's fine, he told himself. He'd performed solo dozens of times in front of packed gymnasiums while involved with the Chinese national gymnastics program. When he put on Airboarding exhibitions he was alone in the limelight, and he enjoyed it. This, he kept reminding himself, was no different.

And yet there was no denying the trickles of sweat that slipped down the back of his neck. He wondered if Hannah could see that.

They had agreed that the forum should be moderated by someone not associated with the Council or a close friend of either candidate. Gina Perotti had volunteered, and the auditorium grew hushed as the dark-haired girl from northern Italy made her way across the stage to one of the two podiums.

"Good evening," she said. "We all know what tonight is about, but let me quickly tell you how it will work."

Gap shifted again in his seat. Even Gina seemed to be completely relaxed. He casually dabbed at another drop of sweat near his temple.

"Two candidates have been nominated for the position of Council Leader: Gap Lee and Hannah Ross. Both candidates understand that this might be only a temporary measure, and have stated their intention to remain in office only until Triana Martell returns to the ship and is deemed fit to hold the position, or until the standard Council elections that take place in about twenty-two months.

"This forum tonight is the first of two; the second will take place on Friday, and the election will be held on Saturday morning. Tonight's agenda is simple; both candidates will have a maximum of ten minutes to make a formal address, then we'll have up to thirty minutes allotted for questions from the crowd. At the end, the candidates will be given five minutes each to summarize and make closing statements. That means everything should be wrapped up in about an hour."

Gap chanced another sideways glance at Hannah. She still

appeared completely unruffled. This time, however, she turned to look back at him and offered a polite smile.

"The order is unimportant," Gina said, "but one name was chosen at random to go first, and that was Gap. So, please welcome our first candidate for the position of Council Leader: Gap Lee."

Polite applause and a few whistles from the back of the room greeted him as he sprang up the steps. He nodded thanks to Gina and made his way to the first podium. He had a momentary flash of standing in this exact spot just a few days ago, addressing the crew, leading them through the first dark hours after Triana disappeared. Tonight was a different story; tonight he was making a sales pitch.

He had debated whether or not to use notes for his presentation and, in the end, opted to take a chance by simply shooting from the hip. He hoped that whatever he lost in crispness would be compensated for by a natural, conversational delivery. He'd heard of politicians long ago delivering what they called "fireside chats," and decided to try a modern version.

Adopting the most relaxed stance he could, he looked out over the faces. "Let me start by saying that I wish we weren't here tonight. I think if we all had our way, Triana would still be our Council Leader, we'd be cruising along with no problems whatsoever, and Channy would give us all two days off each week without running us into the ground."

There was a smattering of laughter, exactly the type of beginning that Gap was looking for.

"But the fact of the matter is that Triana is currently missing, and we have a problem with our radiation shield that is potentially dangerous. With everything that's going on, it's too bad that we also must deal with an election. So, while we know that change is inevitable . . . it doesn't have to be extreme. Tonight I'll show you that a slight adjustment in the Council would make the most sense during a topsy-turvy time. I'm confident that you'll choose leadership experience during a crucial moment in our journey."

Up until this point Gap had memorized what he was going to say. From here on out, however, it would be whatever felt right at the time. For the next few minutes he talked about the trials they'd weathered together, from the stowaway, to the critical encounter around Saturn, and the deadly minefield of the Kuiper Belt. Without directly referencing it, he alluded to the fiery confrontation that had divided the crew during their Kuiper crisis, hoping that it would bring back memories of his victory over Merit on this very stage. Gap believed that it was the strongest card he could play.

But there had been more recent confrontations, he said. These violent altercations jeopardized not only the health of those involved, but potentially the safety of the entire crew. Damages from one of the fights had even put their food supply at risk. This would not be tolerated.

When his ten minutes were up, he thanked the crew for their attention and descended the stairs to his seat on the front row. Gina returned to the microphone.

"Our second candidate for the position of Council Leader is Hannah Ross."

Polite applause spread across the auditorium. To Gap it seemed to represent a combination of courtesy and curiosity.

Hannah apparently had no qualms with using prepared notes.

She placed her workpad on the podium and shyly gazed out at the crew. The first sound she made was a nervous chuckle. Gap couldn't tell if it was intentional or not, but the effect was obvious: the crew smiled back at her, as if they felt the butterflies she must be experiencing. Brilliant, Gap thought. Brilliant.

Hannah looked down at her workpad. "Three years is not a long time, really. Well, three years ago I was coming home from school, looking forward to a quiet evening at home, maybe doing some homework, then a little painting. I remember that I was working on a chalk piece that was a lot of fun, and I was anxious to try to finish it that night.

"I still have the memory of both of my parents waiting for me at the door. They never did that; they were usually off at work when I got home. But there they were. The first thing I thought was, 'Oh no, Grandma's sick again.' I couldn't tell from their faces if they were happy, or sad, or . . . or what. But they brought me inside, sat me down, and told me the news: I had been accepted to the *Galahad* training center. Just like all of you. You probably remember the day you found out, too."

Gap marveled at the way she was connecting emotionally with the crowd. He never knew that she had that skill hidden behind her shy, quiet exterior. He could feel a definite vibe in the air, a feeling that the crew of *Galahad* was collectively embracing Hannah.

"And now," she said, "three years later, I'm not only part of a select group of people who have been chosen to colonize a new world, but I'm standing here tonight, applying for the position of Council Leader." She chuckled again, then added, "And you know what? I never did finish that chalk drawing."

Now a genuine rush of laughter swelled towards the stage. Gap was not immune to her charm either, and found himself laughing as well.

"But that's okay," Hannah said, regaining her control of the room. "I've had some time to pursue my love of art, and a lot of time to do what I love the most: science and mathematics. I'm so lucky to be part of this mission, and to have the galaxy as a laboratory. Believe me, I don't take it for granted.

"I understand that I might not have the Council experience that Gap has, and I also know that I don't necessarily have a dynamic, outgoing personality. I'm aware of all of that. But I hope that, after you get to know me, and get to know my work ethic, you'll support my run for the position of Council Leader. By the time you vote this Saturday morning, I intend to answer any questions about my abilities that you might have."

Solid, Gap decided. Her presentation was honest and straightforward. She didn't hide her lack of leadership experience, and the fact that she addressed her own reputation for being shy turned it to her advantage. He had to admit that he was impressed.

When she finished her opening comments, there was another wave of applause. This time, to Gap's ear, it seemed congratulatory. She acknowledged the response while Gina waved Gap onstage to stand at the other podium.

"And now," Gina said, "as I mentioned, there will be a question and answer period. I know that some of you might want to use this time to show off or try to make everyone laugh, but please, serious questions only. Both Hannah and Gap will have up to two minutes to answer each question."

A handful of arms were raised, and, one by one, crew members stood and addressed the candidates. The first two questions had to do with their views on the mission so far, and their vision for how to handle what might lie ahead. Both Hannah and Gap gave articulate and well-reasoned answers.

From the second row an arm was raised. "There has been some talk going around about both of you sharing the position of Council Leader, since it might only be temporary. Thoughts on that?"

Gap looked over at Hannah to see if she wanted to answer first; she looked back at him. He decided to jump in.

"I haven't heard anything about that," he said. "However, I don't think it's a good idea. Too many times people are so leery of change, or of hurting someone's feelings, that they try to please everyone at the same time. We have to be tougher than that. I obviously respect the abilities that Hannah has, and I hope she feels the same about me. Leadership is about making the tough decisions, whether they're popular or not; it's about being brave enough to stick your neck out, to make a decision based on the facts and what's best for the ship and crew. Believe me, the Council is important, and it's good to have a committee on some things. But in the end, what we need is someone who will stand up and make the call. That's why you elect a Council Leader."

Hannah nodded. "I agree with Gap. I know that some people want everything to always be friendly and smooth. Well, it doesn't always work out that way. If I'm elected Council Leader, I will always want the opinions of Gap, the rest of the Council, and even the feedback from you, the crew. But ultimately a leader makes a call. So, no, I would never advocate sharing a leadership position."

A question was posed about making changes to the rotating work cycles; both Hannah and Gap gave vague answers, mainly because neither thought the issue to be the most critical item they had to deal with at the time.

Finally, the question that had been avoided to this point was posed by Mathias. "I'd like to know what each of you thinks might be causing the problem with the radiation shield, and what you suggest we do about it. And your thoughts on what everyone is calling the space lightning."

It was Gap's turn to go first. He knew that this, of all the issues they faced, was the one which might determine the outcome of the election. He had agonized over the best way to approach it with the crew and knew that it was a tricky proposition. To propose an idea that was unproven, or to suggest something that turned out to be wrong, could be disastrous. On the other hand, to say "I have no idea" would be political suicide.

He looked around the room. It was deadly silent.

"Here's where we stand on the radiation shield problem as of this afternoon," he said. "The power unit which drives the shield continues to randomly drop out, usually for less than one second, but a couple of times now for a little more. I want to start by giving credit to the hard-working team in Engineering. They've voluntarily put in extra hours, and have handled the situation professionally and competently. I couldn't ask for better people to work with side by side.

"I think you all know how serious this could turn out to be. There's always a possibility, of course, that it's something temporary that we'll leave behind as quickly as it started. But we can't automatically assume that. So we approach it in two parts: isolate the problem, then solve it."

He knew that a general answer to the question wouldn't satisfy most of the crew, but still he wanted to tread carefully. Plus, he did his best to put himself in Hannah's shoes and tried to guess how she would respond to the question. He was in the midst of the crisis down in Engineering; what information could she provide without the same access? He wondered if his best position on the issue would be to offer the fewest details possible and trust that Hannah's contribution would be even less. He swallowed hard and charged forward.

"We began by replacing the shield unit itself, and that changed nothing. So, although there's a slight possibility that the problem is internal, it now appears most likely that we're being affected by something outside the ship.

"We've investigated a variety of ideas, and currently we believe that we might be dealing with a phenomenon that we've labeled 'space waves.' These are waves of radiation that are produced naturally in our galaxy but are normally diverted around our solar system by our sun's own energy blast. When these space waves make contact at the extreme edge of our system, they create ripples. *Galahad* is shooting through these ripples, and it's having a negative reaction with our radiation shield."

Gap paused. The crew was completely absorbed in his description. It was a gamble for him to so quickly default to Julya's suggestion of the space waves, but it simply seemed to be the most viable idea so far. From the third row he could see Ruben staring up at him, a worried expression on his face. Ruben had voiced the biggest potential roadblock to the wave theory, the fact that *Galahad* was too far beyond the outer ring of the solar system for the waves to have this effect. But, again, it was the best suggestion so far. Gap ran with it.

However, he knew that the assembled crew members were waiting for the most important detail of all: what to do about it. For that, honesty would have to suffice.

"I'd love to tell you how we combat this problem, but I can't. We're working around the clock and hope to have a solution soon. If it is indeed a wave problem, then one idea is that we develop a method of riding the waves."

"Surfing!" someone shouted from the middle of the room, which prompted a tension-breaking laugh.

"Well," Gap said with a smile, "if that's what it takes, I'm all for it. Those of us who like to Airboard would love it." The other boarders in the room responded with a shout and applause.

"And finally," he said, "I know that we're all curious and a little concerned about the latest mystery to hit us. We just don't have enough information about these intense flashes of light that have struck us twice. We haven't noticed any damage, but we can't say for sure." He shook his head. "Actually, when I say we don't have enough information, the truth is that we don't have *any* information. We see the flash of light, we pick up readings of bizarre particles that we can't identify . . . and that's it. Is it tied to the radiation issue? I wish I knew."

He looked over at Hannah and nodded. He had enormous respect for her scientific mind and was curious to hear what her answer might be. She looked down at her workpad for a long time.

"As some of you know," she said, "I spend most of my free time immersed in the science of our trip. Space fascinates me, always has. I loved our slingshot around Saturn; I was practically obsessed with the possibilities of life on Titan, and then our discovery of the Cassini; and I spent hours trying to solve the mysteries of the Kuiper Belt. All of it, to me, boils down to the pure beauty of mathematics.

"So now, as you can imagine, my focus has been on the radiation problem. I'm not in the trenches with Gap and his team—and believe me, I wish my rotation right now was in Engineering—but the majority of my free time has been consumed by the available data and some spirited discussions with Roc."

Gap felt a twinge of jealousy. Of course Roc was at the disposal of each and every crew member on the ship, but he couldn't help but feel that theirs was a special relationship. To think that the computer might somehow inadvertently aid Hannah in her campaign . . .

"So, do I have a definite answer?" Hannah continued. "No. I certainly don't have a clue about the space lightning. As Gap said, it leaves nothing for us to grab on to. But I do have what I strongly believe to be the most likely cause of our radiation dilemma."

She threw a quick glance at Gap, and he swore that her expression said, "Are you ready for this?" Then, looking back over the packed auditorium, she said, "Although I respect Gap's position, the problem is not caused by space waves. The shield that we rely upon to protect us from this sea of deadly radiation is being shaken apart at the molecular level, as is the rest of the ship, including the engines and life support. We haven't seen those effects yet, but we will."

The crew was shell-shocked. They sat frozen in their seats, staring up at the stage, afraid to utter a sound. Gap waited for a count of ten before deciding to plunge in with a question of his own.

"And what," he said, "is causing this molecular destruction?"

Hannah turned to face him. "The same wormhole that took Triana away from us. It might have folded up and disappeared, but it left behind some significant damage, something that we're still feeling, and will likely have to deal with for a while. I think the best way to describe it is to say that this section of space is bruised."

There was a sudden release of energy in the room as the crew reacted. A loud rumble of voices swallowed the auditorium, with dozens of individual conversations competing with one another. Gap's mouth fell open, and he stared across the stage at Hannah, who stood patiently behind her podium, watching, waiting.

17

Gap sat alone in his room, barefoot, stretching his feet out under his desk. It was after ten o'clock, but there wasn't anywhere on the ship—other than this room, it seemed—that wasn't bustling with activity. The Dining Hall had become the primary spot for people to gather and talk, and the Rec Room was packed. Almost two hours after the forum had come to its electric conclusion, crew members were still fired up to discuss Hannah's explosive theory.

But Gap wanted solitude.

It stung on more than one level. Hannah had laid out a case for what was eating away at their primary radiation defense shield, and she had been very convincing. It was a double blow, because it not only called into question Gap's ability to think through a major crisis, but it undoubtedly elevated Hannah's leadership status in the eyes of the crew.

Not to mention the fact that, if her theory was correct, the ship was being dismantled at a molecular level, which made the election results pointless anyway. It would be a matter of which bullet took them out first: deadly radiation, or the loss of their life-support systems. Neither was pleasant to contemplate.

The few minutes after Hannah's announcement remained a blur to Gap. He had a vague memory of Gina restoring order in the room, but it had taken a while. Both candidates had offered their closing statements, but he honestly couldn't recall if he'd even spoken in complete sentences. His mind had already been racing through the consequences of Hannah's wormhole hypothesis. She, however, had summarized quickly and eloquently, apologizing that she did not—at the moment—have a solution in mind, because she had only just formulated her idea in the last few hours. She would, she promised, be working diligently to find a solution.

As the auditorium emptied, Gap had worked his way through the crowd, back to his room to sift through his troubled thoughts. He had ignored calls from well-wishers; in his mind they were likely only pity calls. Like everyone else, he was well aware that Hannah had convincingly taken round one.

Against his better judgment he decided to engage the ship's computer. "Roc, I suppose you heard Hannah's presentation tonight at the forum."

"It was very exciting," Roc said. "At one point I almost choked on my popcorn."

"I'm sure. But let's talk about this wormhole theory. She said it caused damage in this section of space. The term she used was 'bruised.' What exactly does that mean?"

"It means you probably lost the election."

Gap sighed. "Please, pal, not tonight. Just talk to me about the facts."

"Oh, all right. I have to admit that Hannah's idea is perhaps a bit far-fetched, and maybe even impossible from a physics point of view. But, as we've pointed out countless times, maybe *nothing* is impossible at some level, or in some corner of space. So, having said that, let me try to reduce her very colorful description down to some manageable pieces.

"We know that the wormholes burst open with a sizable bang. Even at a considerable distance they knocked us around pretty well. The same can be said for their very abrupt disappearance. Apparently wormholes are attention hogs, and can't stand to enter or leave a room without everyone noticing.

"We also know that space is really like a piece of fabric. Wait, that's been used a million times; I'm sick of the fabric analogy. Let's say that space is like the palm of your hand. Got that visual? Okay, close your eyes and imagine that your palm is now holding stars and planets and Channy's exotic T-shirts, and all of those things sit in your palm, but they have a lot of mass, so they warp the skin, causing little dents. When scientists say that space is warped, that's what they mean. Or maybe a few of them think that warped space means that space is mentally unstable, but those scientists don't get invited back to the really cool conferences with the colorful name badges and nifty goody bags. Following me so far?"

"It's a challenge, but I'm holding on. Can we get back to the bruises?"

"Okay," Roc said. "Now for a moment imagine the way these wormholes operate. Suddenly, from across the room, a straw races up and punches a hole in the middle of your hand, right up through your palm. Grisly, eh? Blood, tendons, muscle, yecch. Of course it will make your hand jump, because . . . well, it hurts. But the damage goes beyond that. Little blood vessels around the wound are broken, and they end up leaking into the tissue around the wound, and that's why you get a bruise."

Gap sat patiently, taking it all in. "Uh . . . right. I understand the concept of a human bruise. But how does space bruise?"

"We have no idea that it does," Roc said. "In fact, until Hannah first proposed this idea I'd never heard of it before. But I love it. If she turns out to be right, we should create a little fake Nobel Prize necklace and let her walk around with it. The concept is so simple, and yet . . . not. The wormholes are puncturing the skin of space where they pop out."

Gap pinched his lower lip with his fingers. "And the leaking blood? Is that radiation leaking through from the other side of the wormhole?"

"Close your eyes again and this time imagine me shrugging."

"But it's Hannah's best guess, right?"

"Yep," the computer said. "Seeping, oozing radiation. And potent, too. It spreads out around the space where the wormhole blasted through and leaves little concentric circles of energy. We just happen to be skipping through those rings, and they're overwhelming our radiation shield. At least that's the theory."

The concept, Gap had to agree, was brilliant. It might never be proved, or it might even be dead wrong, but it explained almost everything they were experiencing.

Suddenly, a terrifying thought made him sit up straight. "Wait. If the radiation coming through the wormhole is that intense, what does that mean for Triana? She would be right in the middle of that soup on the other side. That would mean . . ." He couldn't finish the sentence. To think of Triana, pummeled by that much energy, was too much.

"I'm not so sure of that," Roc said. "I don't think the radiation spilling out on this side is from one source."

"What does that mean?"

"I'm working on it. Let me give it some thought and I'll get back with you. In the meantime, don't mourn Triana's passing just yet."

In a way, Gap realized, he had gradually been mourning Tree for a long time, long before she took off in the pod. But Roc was right; until they had more information, it was pointless to jump to any conclusions.

"I see that you're deep in thought," the computer said, "and since that's very rare, I'm a little hesitant to interrupt."

"All right, wise guy, what's on your mind?"

"You haven't asked for my opinion, but would you mind if I made a keen observation, followed by an extremely practical suggestion?"

Despite his heavy heart, Gap couldn't help but laugh. "I know you're going to anyway, so I give you permission. What's the observation?"

"You and I have spent many hours together, beginning with your training at Galahad Command. We've weathered difficult times together, we've navigated some tough obstacles along the way, and you even saved my circuits one time, a debt that I have tried to repay by showering you with my knowledge and my charm."

"I'm very grateful for that," Gap said with a smirk.

"The road has not been bumpy the entire route, though. We've also shared some good times, including long, quiet evenings engaged on the battlefield of Masego. You're really improving, by the way."

"Yeah, yeah. You keep saying that so I'll continue to let you stomp me."

"True, but that's not the point," Roc said. "The point is that I probably know you better than anyone on this ship. Which is why I'm able to make the observation that I'm about to make."

"And that is . . . ?"

"You have gone from being an enthusiastic, ever-optimistic, lead-the-charge kind of guy, to a mopey, woe-is-me kind of guy. It's so very unattractive, and it's certainly not you. I noticed it in phases not long after we left Earth and wrote it off to those pesky human hormones. But the phases have been lasting longer, until now, with this election upon us, you seem to be perpetually in a lousy mood. Which is a waste, really, because Bon already placed his flag on that territory long ago, and there's not enough room for both of you."

Gap sat silently, his hands in his lap. He wanted to argue with what Roc was saying, but knew in his heart that he had no case.

"Anyway, that's the observation," Roc said. "And now, for the unsolicited advice, which, if you think about it, might be the best kind of all, because people never ask for advice when they know they're wrong, they only ask when they want someone to tell them what they want to hear. Whew, that's a mouthful—or, in my case, a speakerful—but you get it.

"I strongly recommend that you go back to the Gap who boarded this ship. Yes, Triana is gone, but the crew needs leadership. Yes, we are on the verge of being microwaved like a bag of popcorn, but the crew needs someone with vision. And yes, Hannah smoked you during the first forum, but for your mental health you need to keep your head up and learn.

"And," the computer continued, "I think you'll find that the best therapy for you right now is to take Hannah's theory, or any other plausible idea, and dive right in to solve the problem. So far it seems like you are tiptoeing around the radiation issue, almost like you're afraid to make a wrong step. You're asking for a lot of opinions, a lot of suggestions, yet seem to be unable—or unwilling—to take your own ideas out for a test ride. I think you're taking this 'interim Council Leader' title too seriously, and you're playing too conservatively, as if you're playing not to lose. The old Gap would play to win."

Gap ran a hand through his hair. When he spoke, all he could think to say was: "Wow."

"And that's all the free advice I have for you tonight," Roc said. "Any additional wisdom will be on the clock."

"Wow, that's . . . uh . . ." Gap stared down at his hands for a moment. The words could have stung, but the truth within them seemed to soften them somewhat. Or, more likely, he realized, he knew it all along, and Roc merely vocalized what Gap understood at his core. And yet knowing something doesn't necessarily call one to action; it often takes validation of those thoughts from someone else. In this case, Gap could almost see the sleep-walking version of himself through a veil, shrouded, hidden in shadow. Roc had pulled the veil aside.

Gap grabbed his shoes and stood up. "Thanks, Roc. And I mean that. I know that you're right. Which is difficult for me to say to you, by the way."

"I'm sure."

"But you're right. I mean it, thanks."

"Just part of my job," the computer said. "Beats monitoring the sewage system."

Gap nodded. "Well, if you'll excuse me, I want to check in with the team down in Engineering, and then get some sleep. Got a lot of work to do tomorrow."

He slipped his shoes on, then hustled out the door and down the curved corridor to the lift.

18

That was a thing of beauty," Merit said.

Hannah didn't have to turn and face him; even with her back to him she could guess his pose: leaning against the far wall, arms crossed, a single strand of raven hair hanging across his face. And, of course, the usual wicked grin.

She was back at the secluded window near the Spider bay, driven to find peace and quiet following the mayhem of the forum. She suddenly was the center of attention aboard the ship, and it felt crushing, suffocating. She'd smiled and mumbled thanks to the crowd of well-wishers as she threaded her way out of the auditorium, then quickly slipped away to the lift and the sanctuary of the dim lower level.

Somehow she had known that Merit would be right on her heels.

She finally looked over her shoulder and had to resist the urge to laugh; he stood exactly as she'd pictured him.

"Beauty?" she said. "It was a circus." She turned her attention back to the view through the window. "I should've gone to the Council instead of dropping a bomb like that."

"It would have been a bombshell coming from them, too," Merit said. "What difference does that make?" He walked over and stood next to her. "Of course you're going to second-guess everything right now. But I'm telling you, it was perfect. When the forum began, you were seen as a token opponent, someone simply there to fill out the ballot card. But now you've given this crew the information they needed, and you've showed them that you're more than qualified to lead this mission."

"I didn't give them much 'information,' Merit. I scared them, which is not what I wanted to do."

"They've been through it before."

Hannah shook her head. "The idea that we're being atomically dismantled? Or, if that doesn't do us in first, that we'll be fried by a jet stream of radiation? They haven't been through that before. And yet all you seem to care about is this ridiculous election." She gave him an icy look. "That *is* all you care about, isn't it?"

He crossed his arms again and returned her glare. "Yes," he said. "Or no. Whichever you prefer to hear. But it would be nice if you cared about it a little more."

She rolled her eyes. "Right. Wanting to simply win the election isn't caring; you only really care if you want to completely destroy the other person. Got it."

"You wear me out, Hannah. I came to offer congratulations for a job well done, to compliment you on the way you handled yourself, and for whatever reason you lash out at me. I never said anything about destroying anyone."

"But it's implied in everything you say."

"I can't help what you think," Merit said. "But I'll say it again: you did a terrific job tonight. If you want to lead this ship, you can't feel regret about how well you defeated your opponent. Once you start feeling sympathy, you're doomed. Leaders are strong."

"And I believe leaders have compassion," Hannah said. "Why don't we just agree to disagree on a few things. Now tell me what else you want to talk about, because I'd like some alone time before I fall into bed."

He stared at her for a moment before pushing away from the wall and walking slowly, back and forth, across the corridor. "Well, it's going to be hard for us to strategize on the next forum if we can't agree on tactics. You confuse aggressive campaigning with being cold and heartless. All I'm saying is that if you have Gap down right now, you better put him away. For one thing, you need to point out the breakdown in discipline on the ship in just the short time that Triana's been gone. You need to express that these fights are a sign that Gap's not ready to lead. The damage to the Farms could be a crucial element in all of this. That's a direct reminder of how fragile our ecosystem is."

Hannah scowled but didn't respond. Merit stopped pacing, faced her, and spread his hands. "The crew is ready to follow you after your presentation tonight. They *want* to follow you. You showed them intellect and instinct. But the next thing you have to show them is courage. Courage to make the hard choices, courage to take chances. You have to appear strong. Otherwise they'll simply see you as a resource for Gap, someone he turns to when he needs the facts."

Most of what Merit said rolled off Hannah without an effect, but for some reason this last comment stuck. She didn't mind helping, but to be thought of as merely a smart resource . . .

This was crazy. Merit was playing on her emotional scars, poking where he knew she'd be sensitive. Now he was planting the idea that Gap would only use her for information. But Gap wasn't that way.

Was he?

Her thoughts tumbled out of control. She needed order, but it was out of her grasp. "I have to go," she said, turning from the window but avoiding eye contact with Merit. "I know you want to talk about the next forum, but I can't right now. I need sleep. It's late, I'm tired, and, quite frankly, I'm a little tired of you and your pacing. Let me get some rest and we can pick this back up tomorrow, okay?"

He pulled up in front of her. "Yeah, okay. Get some sleep. I'm sure you're exhausted."

She made an exaggerated show of walking around him to make her way back to the lift. Just before she rounded the turn she heard him call out to her, "You're just a few days away from being elected Council Leader of *Galahad*. Get all the sleep you can."

After tossing and turning all night, Gap was convinced that what he needed more than anything else was a good, solid workout to start his day. Airboarding sounded more appealing, but a strenuous round of Channy's morning routine was probably a better call. He could always try to squeeze in a few laps later at the track.

But first things first. Instead of heading towards the gym on the lower level, he took the lift up to the domes. This might be the best time to reach Bon before activity at the Farms reached its peak. And, after being cooped up in Sick House and his room, it was a sure thing that Bon would already be in his office. Whether he would be in any kind of mood to talk was another matter.

"Bet you're glad to be back at work," Gap said, sticking his head in the office.

Bon was sitting on the floor, surrounded by what looked like crop samples. His workpad was on his lap. He looked up, then returned to his work. "I expected you, but not this early," he said.

Gap sat down in one of the chairs. "Busy day. Thought I might start it off with a social call."

"Yes, that's usually why people come to see me."

Gap smiled. "I see that your face-plant in the crops might have bloodied your lip, but it hasn't stripped you of your sarcastic wit."

"It didn't strengthen my patience, either. I'm here early to catch up on work. What is it you want to talk about?"

"Things have changed since the Council meeting," Gap said. "It was one thing for you to insist on having a private chat with the Cassini when it seemed like you had some measure of control. But even you have to admit that there's no question anymore about how dangerous it is."

"All right, it's dangerous."

Gap realized that this discussion would be no different than most with Bon. In a way it was like soldiers charging a hill, fighting like mad for every foothold, advancing just a few steps at a time, then digging in before clawing their way upward again. With Bon you always had to fight for each step; nothing was given to you.

"Don't you think it's time we also talked about your agenda with the Cassini?" Gap said. "You know I was there, so it's not entirely a mystery anymore."

"Oh?" Bon said. "And what exactly did you hear?"

"I heard you asking a question: 'Where is she?' "

Bon said nothing and punched in some figures on his workpad.

"If you're looking for Tree, why can't you talk to the rest of the Council about that?" Gap said. "Why the secrecy? Why is that something you need to do on your own? Are you trying to be a hero or something?"

Bon rolled his eyes. "Yes, that must be it. That sounds just like me, doesn't it?"

"You're giving me nothing!" Gap said, his voice rising. "If you're irritated by people always trying to guess your motives and your emotions, quit playing these silly games. The whole 'dark and mysterious' act has worn pretty thin. I'll stop guessing as soon as you tell me what the answer is."

Bon set his workpad on the floor and stood up, brushing off his pants. He walked over to his desk and sat down. "I think you might have misunderstood what was going on."

Gap fought to control his anger. He turned to look out the window into Dome 1 and mentally counted to ten. "All right, then make it clear to me."

Bon shrugged. "It's not even clear to me. When we connect, they direct most of the conversation. I get in questions only when I'm able to fight back their power. That's why the connections seem so violent to an outsider."

"I already know that," Gap said. "You're avoiding the question."

"I'm not sure how to answer your question. I told you the last time we had this chat, it's personal."

Gap stood up and went to the window. He leaned against the

sill and stared back at Bon. "Okay, then tell me this. Did they answer you?"

Bon sat quietly for a moment, tapping an index finger on his desk. "It's not always easy to decipher their answers."

"But they did answer you?"

"In a way. But you don't understand, they don't exactly carry on conversations the way you're used to. It's not a question and answer session. If they respond—*if*—it's more like them implanting a solution somewhere within my brain. I'm not always sure what it means."

Gap nodded thoughtfully. "Like the code they gave you to maneuver through the Kuiper Belt."

"Yeah. When I sat down at the keyboard in the Control Room, I didn't fully understand what I was inputting; it was there, and somehow I accessed it enough to type it in. But if I was given an essay test, I wouldn't know where to begin.

"They're not making me smarter," Bon continued. "It's like they're . . . like they're lending me information. Or maybe a better way to put it is, I'm a courier for the information. I carry it, but it doesn't belong to me."

The concept sounded so alien to Gap. But, he realized, they were dealing with a thoroughly alien entity, one that was comprised almost entirely of thought.

"All right," he said. "But for now the courier service is going on hold. Until Lita's test results come back, no more links. Period." He walked over to the desk and held out his hand. "In fact, let's avoid any more arguments. Give me the translator."

Bon blinked up at him. "What?"

"You heard me. Please, no arguing. Just hand it over."

"I don't have it."

Gap lowered his hand and sighed. "All right, take me to that clearing and let's pick it up. I could probably find my way there eventually, but I don't feel like searching. Let's go."

"It's not there," Bon said with a puzzled look. "I thought you had it already."

"Is this another game?"

"I don't have it," Bon said again. His tone, and the look on his face, convinced Gap that he was telling the truth.

The two were silent for a full minute, eyeing each other. Gap turned to look out the large window into the dome. "One of the workers, perhaps? Have you asked around?"

"It's early; I'm waiting for them to show up. I would imagine that if one of them stumbled across it, they'll bring it to me this morning."

"And you'd rather not just send a mass e-mail to them?"

Bon shook his head. "Let's just say I'd rather not advertise the fact that it's missing." He paused, then leaned back in his chair and said, "It'll turn up."

19

By late Friday afternoon the ship's radiation shield had sputtered five more times, and the crew was visibly on edge. One of the failures spanned almost three seconds, and the general consensus was that a full-fledged collapse might happen at any time.

Gap alternated his attention between solving that problem and preparing for the final election forum. Hannah's bruise theory had captured the imagination of most crew members, and it seemed that the election results might very well depend upon whoever came up with the best solution. Gap had climbed out of bed before six to start in again, and now felt worn down physically. But he remained optimistic.

Optimistic despite the disturbing post he'd seen when he logged on to his computer around noon.

Anyone could post to the community page, and had the option to do so anonymously. Occasional unsigned posts made their way to the main screen, usually to voice minor gripes or suggestions, but they were rare; the general feeling was that anonymous posts carried far less credibility. This particular post grabbed attention with its title: Exploring the Bruise.

Taking up almost two full pages, it allegedly had been submitted by *Friends of Hannah*, and began by recapping her description of the wormholes' effect on space. What followed was grim. Several paragraphs detailed the damage that *Galahad* was experiencing, using terms such as *critical, dire,* and *deadly*. The post also went on to claim that the same destructive force was slowly attacking their own bodies, as well. One particular passage stood out:

> Like an invisible cancer, the sheer corrosive power of the galaxy's radiation is slowly, but inevitably, tearing down our protective walls. How much longer can we stand the assault? We need a leader who can not only find the answers, but keep order among a crew that is obviously unraveling.

Time, the post went on to add, was not a luxury at this point. The crew owed a debt of thanks to Hannah for quickly bringing the issue to their attention, and hopefully she would lead the charge to finding a solution. Otherwise, the authors predicted, both the ship and the crew would be atomically ripped to shreds.

Gap read with interest, aware that the writers—whoever *Friends of Hannah* might be—were responsible enough to close their post with a footnote that stated it was all simply theory. But, tucked quietly within the final lines, the disclaimer was all but lost in the white noise of fear.

He refused to let the post drag him down, even the insinuation that his lack of leadership was responsible for the violence that had broken out. Roc's charge that he pull himself up from the doldrums and concentrate on finding a cure for the ship's ills had rejuvenated him. Even when he overheard workers in the Engineering section talking about Hannah and her sparkling performance at the first forum, he used it as motivation. Now, as the time neared for his next opportunity on stage, he ignored the anonymous propaganda, put his head down, and bulled forward.

And it felt good.

With an hour to go before the forum, he finished the work in his office and rushed up to his room to spend a few moments in quiet meditation. Sitting in semi-darkness with his legs crossed and eyes closed, he drifted in the low sprinkling of traditional Chinese music that filtered through the speakers. For nearly ten minutes he regulated his breathing, inhaling deeply, holding it for several seconds, and then slowly exhaling. He allowed his mind to drain all of the stress and frenzied activity of the day, and soon he could almost smell the mixture of grasses and tree blossoms from the meadow in which he imagined himself.

Then, without a warning of any kind, the mood was shattered.

"Are there lyrics to that song you're listening to?" Roc said. "You certainly can't dance to it—not that I want you to, that would be devastating to watch—and it doesn't seem likely to inspire one to amazing athletic feats, like running backward through cones, or juggling flaming bowling pins. I'm hoping that the lyrics mean something profound. Like 'I Might Be Missing You, But I'm Really Not Looking That Hard.' Something like that."

Gap wanted to be angry for the interruption, but instead caught himself laughing. "I don't think this one has lyrics. It's meant to be soothing and relaxing."

"Makes me want to slam my head in a car door," the computer said. "Which would be outrageous on two levels. One, we have no cars on the ship, and two, I don't have a head."

"Let's put aside the fact that I really don't care if you like this music or not," Gap said. "I'm sure there's a legitimate reason for you to bust in like this, when you know I have a big presentation in—" He squinted over towards the clock on his desk vidscreen. "—in thirty-six minutes."

"It's completely legitimate. You asked earlier for some calculations, and I've downloaded them into your workpad."

Gap straightened out his legs, leaned back into one of his favorite yoga poses, then pushed himself to his feet and walked over to the desk. He flipped through various screens on his workpad until he came to the file he was looking for. After a minute of concentration, he nodded.

"That's great. Thank you, Roc."

"How do you think the crew will take to your suggestion based on these figures?" the computer said.

"Oh . . ." Gap stretched again. "I'd say that a third will support it, a third will be skeptical, and a third will have to go and think about it. Pretty typical."

"Well, good luck," Roc said. "There's an old theater custom on Earth to tell the actors to 'break a leg.' It doesn't mean to literally break your leg, but in your case it might be a great idea. That way you could get pity votes, and after the other night you might need them. Look at Rico; he broke his arm doing something stupid like falling out of the bleachers, and the girls are still all over him. Can you break something in the next few minutes? Even a hairline fracture might be enough."

"Lucky me," Gap said, "to be traveling across the galaxy at near the speed of light with the world's first electronic comedian.

Why don't you go compile a list of prime numbers for a few hours?"

"Don't forget to comb your hair," the computer said.

Thirty minutes later Gap walked into the auditorium. Once again it was almost full, with the only empty seats explained by the crew members who were on mandatory work duty. Hannah was in her same seat; she nodded politely to him, and in return he flashed a large smile.

Once again Gina climbed to the stage to address the crew. She stood at a small podium set off to the side of the stage.

"Welcome to the second—and final—election forum. Tonight we have a slightly different format. Our two candidates for the position of Council Leader will begin with prepared opening statements, but the remainder of the forum will consist of questions that I, as the moderator, have prepared for the evening. Afterward, the candidates will have three minutes to summarize their points and positions.

"I think you're all aware of the procedures for tomorrow's election, but if you have any questions you'll find the information available on your workpad or the vidscreen in your room. Please remember to cast your ballot on your vidscreen prior to three o'clock; no exceptions. Results will be announced at six tomorrow evening."

There was a hum of conversation across the room, and Gina waited patiently for it to die down. "The candidates have agreed that since Gap went first the other night, Hannah would have the honors this evening. So please welcome our two crew members vying for the position of *Galahad* Council Leader: Hannah Ross and Gap Lee."

They walked up the stairs and to their respective podiums together, each acknowledging the applause from the crowd. After taking two deep breaths—and, Gap noticed, aligning her workpad so that it was flush with the edge of the podium—Hannah began her opening statement. She addressed the need for unity, regardless of the outcome of the election, and vowed to remain an enthusiastic and productive member of the crew no matter what results were posted.

Gap noted that she made no mention whatsoever of the anonymous post, nor any mention of the theory that had electrified the crew only two nights earlier. Apparently she was content to wait until the inevitable questions from Gina regarding the possible solution. Her remarks were brief and to the point, and she finished in less than two minutes.

All eyes turned to Gap. He began with his head lowered, staring at an invisible spot on the podium. "It has occurred to me that what we're asking you to do in the next twenty-four hours is predict the future. This thought came to me while I was thinking about the two crew members who began this journey with us, but aren't here tonight.

"Alexa was blessed—although many times she felt she was cursed—with the ability to see the future. It frightened her most of the time, as it probably would any of us. Triana believed that she saw our future, too, and because of that she chose to risk her life to give the rest of us a fighting chance. And I think it's a safe bet that when she plunged into that wormhole, she was frightened as well."

Gap finally raised his head and looked out across the room. "You're being asked to evaluate Hannah, and to evaluate me. Your job is to not only gauge what you hear from us tonight, but to also predict the future. One of us will soon take charge of this mission, and will be responsible for decisions that our lives depend upon. That in itself would normally make anyone frightened.

"But you know what? We've lived with fear too much in the last year. I don't want to live that way anymore. I'm challenging all of you tonight to take the time to really consider what you're going to hear from both of us tonight, and instead of making a decision based on fear, make your decision based on faith."

He let the words sink in, and saw several crew members turn to look at their neighbors.

"In this case," he continued, "I'm not talking about religious or spiritual faith, although many of you will call upon that as well. I'm talking about faith in yourself, faith in your fellow crew members, and faith in the mission itself. We all have to devote the next stretch of our journey to making positive steps forward, to solving our problems through cooperation and hard work, and to shoving aside the fear that has stalked us for too long. All of that will require faith that we summon from deep inside.

"And, when it comes time to predict our future, to predict which candidate will be best suited to lead this crew to Eos, you won't be making your choice from a position of weakness, but rather an incredible position of strength. I, like everyone else, originally viewed this election with sadness because of the disappearance of Triana. But today I realized that we can use this election as a turning point, a red-letter day where we used the sacrifices of our missing comrades to climb higher and reach farther. Thank you."

There was silence at first, then a rolling wave of applause. It was obvious that his words had sparked something within them, and they showed their appreciation.

Gina raised her hands and brought the room back to order. She began the question-and-answer session by asking the candidates to explain their leadership styles and to outline their vision of the Council's responsibility to the crew. Hannah and Gap each gave thoughtful responses. Gap wondered if Hannah would draw upon any of the comments he'd made during their conversation in the Dining Hall, when she had questioned him about his leadership style. But she steered away from that, forging her own way without any reference to that discussion.

The next two questions revolved around crew duties and departmental procedures, both of which were important, and yet not what the assembled crew had come to hear. It wasn't until the fourth question that the crowd sat forward in their seats.

"Gap," Gina said, "we find ourselves in yet another critical situation. Besides the space lightning that has erupted, our ship's radiation shield has failed numerous times. Although it's lasted no more than a few seconds, the potential exists for complete failure, which would ultimately spell doom for this crew. More than a few theories have surfaced as to what might be causing the problem, but I think it's safe to say that many people feel strongly that Hannah's theory of bruised space, caused by the wormholes, might be the leading candidate. If that's the case, what steps would you take as the Council Leader to protect the safety of the ship and crew?"

Gap didn't hesitate; a lull before his answer might give the impression that he was unsure, and he wanted the crew to feel the same confidence that simmered within him.

"I first want to acknowledge Hannah's impressive work on this problem. Obviously we don't know for certain what's causing the radiation shield to fail, but her bruised space theory is a strong possibility. I'm willing to focus our energies on that angle unless, or until, a better idea is presented.

"It's tricky, because we don't know exactly how a bruise affects the fabric of space. We assume that it has caused ripples, or, to use a more descriptive analogy, old-fashioned speed bumps. Our ship is ignoring the speed limit through these speed bumps, which is wreaking havoc and causing major damage."

He took a deep breath and for the first time looked at his workpad. "I believe that our radiation shield is fundamentally sound, which is why it has weathered the storm so far. However, it needs to be turbo-charged. My plan is to transfer energy from the ion power drive of *Galahad* and divert it into a new and improved shield, one that can withstand the shock waves associated with the wormhole's bruise."

Gap saw many of the crew members in the audience nodding their heads in approval. At the same time, out of the corner of his eye, he watched Hannah immediately take up her stylus pen and begin to make notes on her workpad.

"This power diversion, which can be done relatively quickly, will reinforce the shields, effectively tripling the magnetic force that precedes the ship through space. However, I will tell you up front, this diversion comes at a price. And it's a heavy price."

He once again had everyone's full attention.

"Because of the loss of power to our system's drive, our gradual increase in speed will deteriorate. We're assuming that this will be temporary, even though we have no idea the extent of the bruise; once we're in the clear, we should be able to once again revert to our original power output.

"All of this means that our trip will be extended by approximately . . . two years."

There was an immediate reaction from the room. Gap stood back and pretended to scan his notes while loud conversations and arguments broke out. It took Gina more than a minute to calm everyone down. When she had done so, she asked Gap if he wanted to add anything else.

He gazed back across the sea of faces. "I realize that it's not a popular choice, but it's the one that I think gives us the best chance to survive the danger we're facing. I'll post all of the figures right after this forum, and you're free to check them on your workpad or vidscreen."

Another low rumble spread across the auditorium, and Gina held up her hands to prevent it from building. Once it was quiet again, she turned to Hannah.

"Per the rules of this forum, you're permitted to address Gap's plan, and to question him if you like. Then I'd like for you to present your own position, and Gap will be allowed the same follow-up."

Hannah looked over the notes she had hastily scribbled. "I'm intrigued by Gap's idea. However . . ." She paused. "I'm not sure an increase in power to the shields is the answer. As he stated, there's so much we don't know about all of this. But I tend to look at the bruise a little differently. I think of it as a disruption in the very particles that make up space; powering our way through that disruption might have the effect of actually speeding up the damage."

She waited a moment, and then shook her head. "It's an interesting suggestion, I'll leave it at that. I've also given a lot of thought to how we might overcome this problem, and rather than turbocharging the shields, I think our best solution would be to avoid the bruise altogether.

"Again, there are plenty of unknowns. But I think the damage to space could very well be two-dimensional. Consider a normal bruise on your skin: it has length and width as it extends across your body, but rarely lacks any depth. It doesn't extend down into your body very much at all. I believe the wormhole has created the same type of injury to this portion of space. It likely has length and width, but not depth.

"Therefore," she said, "I propose that Galahad be reprogrammed to drop out of the galactic plane, dip under the damaged space, and then resurface after we have traveled out beyond the scope of the bruise."

There was a murmur from the crew as they visualized what Hannah was describing. Gap found himself doing the same, looking down at his hand and imagining a bruise, and how he might dip beneath it.

Hannah cleared her throat and continued. "Gap was up-front with you and told you that his plan might add two years to our journey. My solution also comes at a cost. Because we don't know how deep this bruise extends, or how far along our path to Eos, we could potentially face a delay of perhaps one year."

Rather than put any punctuation on her suggestion, she looked over at Gina to indicate that she was finished. Gina said, "Gap?"

"Well," he began, then chuckled. "Maybe now you all want to vote for 'none of the above.'" A chorus of nervous laughter greeted this.

"I appreciate what Hannah had to say about my plan, and I will start by echoing the same sentiments about hers. It's an interesting idea, and might very well be the way to go. But I guess I go back to the faith I mentioned earlier. I believe that our shields are strong enough, and the basic science behind them is sound enough, to protect us from the damage. Dropping out of our flight path, however, is not a choice I would make. There are too many unknowns. For one thing, we have no proof whatsoever that the bruise is flat; the wormhole could just as easily have ruptured space, exploding outward in all directions. If that's the case, we would still be in the same position, but without the benefit of the added protection I'm proposing.

"There's another potential problem," he added. "Her solution might be quicker, but dropping below the galactic plane could potentially expose us to additional sources of radiation, such as gamma rays. We're shielded somewhat within the cocoon of the Milky Way."

He could see the crew's faces contorting as they wrestled with the two choices now placed before them. Each had pros and cons, and each came with a price tag.

"Before we walk out of here," Gap said, "I would like to thank Hannah for her opening comment about working together, regardless of the outcome. I think you can count on that from both of us."

There was a smattering of applause which slowly built into a crescendo. Hannah and Gap met at the center of the stage and shook hands, then walked down the steps and took their seats in the front row.

"Thank you all for your attention tonight," Gina said to the crowd. "You have plenty to think about. However, I think it's fair to say that both candidates are strong choices. If anything, you should feel good that the ship is in such capable hands. Take some time to consider everything you've heard, and then get a good night's sleep.

"Tomorrow is the first election day on *Galahad*. Good luck to the candidates, and good luck to us all."

20

Lita had never seen the Dining Hall so empty in the morning. It puzzled her, because, if anything, she had expected the room to be packed. Traditionally, during times of stress, people chose to gather around food, to exchange ideas and provide support. For some reason, the crew of *Galahad* had chosen to spend their first election day on their own. She thought it over and decided that the second election forum had shifted the crew's collective mind-set. The poise and style exhibited by both Gap and Hannah had instilled a renewed sense of purpose; the usual gossip and chatter had been replaced by a thoughtful respect of their mission, and their destiny.

This crew, Lita decided, had grown up.

She watched Channy stroll into the room, exchange greetings with a handful of people near the door, then pick up a glass of juice and an energy bar, and wander back to Lita's table.

"Dead in here," Channy said.

"Yeah," Lita said. "I would have stayed in myself, but I thought it would be better if the Council was visible today." She laughed. "Guess it wouldn't have really mattered."

"Tell me about it. The gym was like a ghost town. Wasn't even worth getting up early. Of course, getting up wasn't a problem, really; I hardly slept last night. You?"

Lita shook her head. "I couldn't shut my mind off. The funny thing is, it wasn't about the election, or the radiation problem. I spent most of the night thinking about Triana."

Channy sipped her juice. "Why is that, do you think?"

"I think the election is making everything hit home for me. In a way it was easy to pretend that Triana wasn't really gone, that she would walk in and join us for breakfast like she used to do. Now we're electing her replacement; that's a little too real, you know?"

"Stop it, you're gonna make me cry again," Channy said. "I'm trying to get through today without having a breakdown." She quickly took another sip of juice, blinking hard. After looking around the room, she said, "I voted first thing this morning. I didn't want to have to think about it anymore today. Too draining. What about you?"

Lita smiled at her. "No, I wanted to come down here and just relax a bit. It's been such a bizarre week. I'll head back to the room when I leave here and take care of it. So . . ." She swirled her own glass of juice. "I guess last night must have made some kind of impact on you since you were so quick to cast your ballot."

A sly smile crossed Channy's face. "Let's just say that I'd made up my mind by the time I went to bed. And I know I shouldn't tell you how I voted, but—"

"No," Lita said. "I don't want to know. And don't hint, either. I really don't want to know."

"Oh, you're horrible!" Channy said with a grin. "I'm about to burst."

"Go back to the gym and work it out with some sweat. Now."

Channy laughed. "You're no fun." She reached out and touched the charcoal-colored stone that hung from a simple silver strand around Lita's neck. "Hey, this is gorgeous. How have I not seen it before?"

"It was a gift from Alexa."

Channy gawked. "Alexa?"

Lita related the story of her visit with Katarina, then said, "Alexa kept it tucked away in a box, but I felt like I could honor her by wearing it. Since Nung loves to work with jewelry, I asked what he could do with it, and this is what he brought to me."

"I love it," Channy said. "I'm gonna have to get Nung to make something pretty for me, too." She stood up. "All right, off I go. Let's get together tonight after the results are posted, okay?"

"You have a date."

Channy walked out of the Dining Hall, and Lita fell back into her thoughts of Triana. How would *she* vote? Which candidate would Triana think was the best choice to lead the crew? Gap brought Council experience and good people skills. Hannah brought fresh ideas and a razor-sharp mind for solving problems. Which one would Triana feel should be her replacement?

Lita's head was down, and it took a moment for her to realize that she had company again. Looking up, she was startled to find Bon staring down at her with his cobalt-blue eyes.

"Oh" was the first sound that escaped from her. "Sorry, I didn't hear you walk up."

"I'd like to get the translator back from you, if you don't mind."

Lita blinked. "And good morning to you, too."

"Right."

She couldn't help but laugh. "I know a lot of people have a hard time handling your personality, Bon, including me sometimes. But other times—like right now—it's exactly what I need. Thank you."

He grunted. "Let's talk about the translator."

"What makes you think I have it?"

"Are we really going to go back and forth like this? Wouldn't it save time to just go get it and give it back to me?"

Lita drummed her fingers on the table and found it hard to scrub the smile off her face. "Okay. Yes, I have the translator."

"Of course you do. As soon as I found out that Gap didn't take it, I knew it had to be you. The only thing I don't know is how you knew where to look for it."

"Really? Think about it," Lita said.

Bon stood above her, staring into her eyes. A moment later he nodded once. "Alexa."

"She was one of my best friends, Bon. Girls talk, you know?"

He remained silent and motionless for a moment, then pulled out a chair and sat down across from her.

"I know you pride yourself on being cool and in control," Lita said. "But not everyone is like that. Alexa cared for you a great deal. She wanted to open up so much to you, but never felt like you reciprocated. She wanted someone to talk to about all of those feelings, so she turned to me. I didn't know exactly where the clearing was, but I knew enough to figure it out."

Bon pursed his lips. "So this is a critique of how I handled things with Alexa?"

"No. You are who you are. But I think you regret how you handled things with her. For that matter, I think you regret how you handled things with Triana. I don't know what it was, but something was going on between you two. So no, I'm not going to criticize you; with both of them gone, I can't imagine anyone on this ship more tortured than you. I cared for them both, but at least they knew that."

He turned his head and stared across the room. Lita wondered if it was just the play of the lights, or if his eyes were truly moist.

Finally he looked back at her. "Let's talk about the translator. Are you going to give it back to me?"

"Let's wait until the election is over and we have a new Council Leader. That was my position in the first place. Unless you want to tell me what you're trying to learn from the Cassini."

She thought he might argue with her, but apparently he understood that it was pointless. "All right," he said, and stood up.

And that was it. He spun on his heel and stalked out of the room. Once again Lita had an entire section of the Dining Hall to herself. She took a sip of juice and gazed across the room.

Bon was reluctant to open up to anyone, it seemed. And yet he was willing to allow the Cassini access to his mind, to his thoughts. It was easier for him to form a connection with an alien intelligence than with someone he might actually have feelings for. Why? Was it safer for him somehow?

She rested her head on one hand and glanced back at the door. What was Bon looking for?

* * *

Gap had suggested that Hannah meet him near the window on the lower level, but that spot held too many painful memories for her. Instead they met in the deserted Conference Room. It was a few minutes past noon.

"Thanks for coming," he said.

"Sure." Hannah took a seat at the table. At first Gap considered walking around to the other side so they could face each other, but he elected to sit next to her.

"I heard that we've had two more shield failures today," Hannah said. "How long this time?"

"Both about two seconds," Gap said. "They're fairly regular now. If your theory is correct, little pieces of us are being sliced away each day." He shuddered. "Ugh, what a thought. After reading that post from your friends, I'm sure everyone on the ship is having the same nightmares about it, too."

A shadow crossed Hannah's face. "Listen, those were not my words. You understand that, right? I had nothing to do with that post. I would never endorse that kind of fearmongering. And I would never question . . . well, let's just say that I have no doubt about your leadership skills."

Gap smiled at her. "I know that. But apparently some of your supporters do. Know who it was?"

"No, but I think I have an idea."

There was silence for a few moments before Gap filled the space. "Even if their description is true, what really makes it strange is the fact that we don't feel any different, you know?"

"Yes, but the ship is . . . different today," Hannah said. "I don't know if you've been out much, but there's a strange feeling in the air."

"Yeah, I noticed it, too. It's never been this quiet."

She nodded. "Makes me wish that the day would rush by. I don't know about you, but I'm mentally exhausted."

Gap agreed. While she was talking, he couldn't help but stare at her. Something was different in the way she carried herself, the way she talked. When they were together as a couple she'd been relatively shy and reserved; their energy had been polar opposites. Now there was no doubt in his mind that Hannah had changed. She wasn't necessarily more outgoing, but she exuded a confidence that he'd never seen before. It came across as strength.

Was it a result of the election? Had the forums, along with the vocal support of so many crew members, bolstered her self-image? Or was it more than that? He wondered if it might have been the breakup itself that had shifted something within her. Or . . .

Or could it be that Hannah was involved with someone else? What if her head had been turned by someone new, and the rebound had instilled a shot of confidence?

Gap realized with a start how much that shook him. Since their split he had considered talking to her, trying to mend their differences, perhaps even trying again; he hadn't considered the possibility of her moving on, of her falling for someone else.

Stop it, he told himself. This isn't the time to worry about that.

Almost a minute of silence had passed between them, and Hannah raised her eyebrows. "So, you wanted to talk about something?"

"Oh . . . yeah, I did. Well, nothing major, but . . ." He smiled sheepishly. "Listen, all I wanted to do was have a moment with you in private to wish you good luck. You've impressed everyone on the ship. Especially me."

"Thank you," she said, looking down, a touch of the old Hannah surfacing. "This has been exciting, but also . . ." She seemed to search for the right word. "Difficult. For a variety of reasons."

He stared at her again. "Care to list them?"

Hannah took a quick glance at him, then back at the table, then turned and gazed out the Conference Room's window into space. For a moment she seemed lost among the stars.

"It hasn't been in my nature to get up in front of people and try to lead," she said. "I've generally liked to stay behind the scenes and do the research. So this was a difficult transition.

"It's also difficult because thoughts of Triana keep popping into my head. I had so much respect for her, for the job she did, for the way she handled all of the emergencies that we've faced since we left Earth. And I wondered, am I capable of filling her shoes? Do I have the same strengths that she had?"

"You don't need to have the same strengths," Gap said softly. "Each person leads in their own way. You have your own strengths, you know."

"That's sweet of you to say, but I'm sure you've had the same thoughts," Hannah said. "I almost felt . . . I don't know, unworthy. Unworthy to try to follow the job that Triana did. I mean, whoever takes this position will automatically be judged by the way Triana led this crew. It's been hard coming to grips with the fact that I might soon be under an incredibly strong microscope. As the week has progressed, though, I've begun to realize that anyone would feel out of their league. Triana must have battled the same feelings; why should I be any different?"

Gap understood completely, but said nothing.

"And it's also been challenging on a much more personal level," she said. She turned her head from the window and looked into Gap's eyes. "It's been hard going up against you, Gap. Because . . ."

Her voice trailed off, and her shoulders slumped. As strong as she had seemed a minute earlier, she now seemed emotionally burdened. Gap wanted to reach over and put a hand on her shoulder but thought it might seem condescending.

"Because why?" he said.

She kept her gaze focused on him, something that she might not have pulled off a month or two ago. "Two reasons. First, I've had to promise myself that this would never be about striking back at you for the way things ended. And I won't lie; that's been tough. But I've kept my focus on the position itself, and the fact that there's more to me than you ever were aware of. Yes, you hurt me, but I won't let that define me. I'm worth more than that. I'm aware of it, and the crew is slowly becoming aware of it. When I started this I think I really wanted you to be aware of it, too. Now I'm not sure that's as important to me anymore."

Gap felt as if he'd been pushed backward. He fought to keep his composure, willing himself to not show weakness in front of her.

Nodding slightly, he said, "And the other reason this has been difficult?"

She paused a moment before answering. "Because I still care about you, that's why."

He felt his breath catch in his throat. Although he might

have thought about it, he never thought he'd hear her say it. There was another long moment of silence. Finally, he reached over and placed his hand on top of hers.

"And I still care about you, Hannah. This . . . this has been hard for me, too."

What happened next surprised him. She suddenly pulled her hand out from under his and stood up. "But I don't want to feel this way," she said. "Do you understand me? I fight with this every day. I've told myself that I need to move on, that you're not right for me. Anyone who would dump me the way you did . . ." Her eyes narrowed and she pointed a finger towards him. "I don't want to feel this way. And I can't even believe I told you that I cared."

She turned and took a few steps towards the door, then turned back to face him. "I'm sure this gives you some sort of satisfaction, and that makes me even more angry at myself."

"Hannah," he said, standing and taking a step towards her. "No, don't say that. It doesn't give me—"

She put a hand on his chest to stop him. "Forget I said anything," she said. "Just forget everything I've said in the last minute. Thank you for the good-luck wishes. Same to you."

It looked as though she wanted to add something else, but it never made it out. She cut off what sounded like a sob, pulled her head back high, and gave him a defiant look before striding out of the room.

21

By now you know what a keen observer I am when it comes to human interaction and psychology. If you don't know it by now, go back to the first volume, start over, and read every word up to this point until you say, "Oh yeah, that Roc is a keen observer."

Or save yourself some time and just concede the point.

Anyway, the reason I bring this up is because I've noticed how difficult it can be for some people to confront others when they discover the truth about them.

Maybe confront is too strong of a word; how about "bring it to their attention"?

Regardless, I believe the average person would rather let it go and not make waves. But, because of that, it also means you have an entire subset of people who KNOW that people won't call them on something, and so they learn to therefore take advantage of the situation.

Does that make sense? No? Apparently you're not as keen of an observer as I am, but don't let that get you down. Just consider this: Bon seems to keep a lot of secrets tucked away behind a screen that's coated with a gruff varnish. Most people are too intimidated

*to even poke around behind that screen, which is probably what
he's counting on.*

*But not Lita. Remember what I said about her profound thinking?
This girl is all about the truth.*

The late afternoon irrigation schedule was underway, so as
Lita walked out of the lift into Dome 1 she inhaled the humid air and immediately imagined a sunny day on the beach
near her home in Veracruz. The salty sea air had always invigo-
rated her. Now, when she was fortunate enough to experience a
similar feeling in *Galahad's* domed Farms, she instantly thought
of home.

Splashing across the coarse sand at the water's edge, listening
to the roar as the late-day waves relentlessly pounded the coast-
line, she could never stifle a laugh. This, to her, was the ultimate
expression of Earth's life cycle. Land that had furiously burst from
the ocean floor, courtesy of the planet's tectonic convulsions, was
then gradually torn apart, one wave at a time. Wave after wave,
year after year, for eons. The ocean fought to wear down the con-
tinent that had pushed it aside, to get the final word in the tug-of-
war between sea and sand . . . only to have the process begin
anew with another volcanic eruption.

It was one of the reasons she kept the small glass cube on her
desk in Sick House. It was not only a reminder of home, but a
reminder of the universe's cyclical dance. It seemed one force
always sought to wear down another.

Galahad was running head-on into its own waves.

As she approached Bon's office she saw him exit and begin to
march down a trail towards the far side of the dome. She quickened

her pace to catch him, reluctant to call out his name until she got closer. Like everything else about him, however, Bon's stride was determined and intense. They were deep into a field of potatoes, the path cutting diagonally across the crop, when she closed to within thirty feet of him.

"Bon, hold up a second," she said, winded.

He stopped and turned, mild surprise on his face. "What are you doing here?"

Lita covered the distance between them and stood with her hands on her hips, trying not to show him how hard she was breathing. "We need to finish our discussion."

"Why? You don't seem open to negotiation on the subject."

"I might surprise you," she said. "Is there someplace nearby where we can sit down and talk?"

Bon gestured with his head. "Up ahead. It's where I'm going anyway, another irrigation pump that's acting up. Again."

She ignored his irritation and pointed down the path. "After you."

Two minutes later they crossed over into a grove of fruit trees, and soon after that came upon the gray irrigation pump box. Beside it was a small bench. Lita sat down, while Bon leaned against the box.

"Well?" he said.

"I've been doing some thinking about you and your stubborn refusal to talk to us about this." She reached into a pocket and pulled out the translator. She noticed that Bon's eyes grew wide for a split second, then he crossed his arms and appeared nonchalant.

"It didn't make sense to me for a long time," Lita continued. "I heard about your request to the Cassini: 'Where is she?' you said. Well, why wouldn't you want us to know about that? Why wouldn't you want our help? We all care about Triana, we're all scared to death about what's happened to her, and we all want her back. I've always felt, like I told you, that there was something between you two, but I don't think even you knew exactly what that was."

She paused and leaned forward, resting her elbows on her knees.

"So why, I wondered over and over again, would you possibly want to do a search for her without including us? If the Cassini were able to help, we would eventually have to be brought into it at some point. So why shut us out?"

Bon shifted his weight but kept his arms crossed, the classic pose of defensiveness and stonewalling. Lita knew he would offer nothing in return to her questions. He blinked once or twice.

"And then, after we spoke in the Dining Hall, I did some thinking. It slowly dawned on me that I was dead wrong about your connection. In fact, we were all wrong, weren't we?"

"I'm afraid I don't know what you mean," he said.

A slow smile spread across Lita's face. "Yes, you do. And I'd appreciate it if you'd stop the games. All of us were a bit surprised when we thought you were using the link to probe the galaxy, looking for Triana. I mean, it's touching . . . but it's not what you were doing."

"And what was I doing?"

Lita paused before saying, "Looking for Alexa."

For what seemed an eternity they stared at each other without moving, without uttering another sound. At last Bon broke eye contact and turned his head to look back down the path they'd walked. Lita nodded slowly.

"Uh-huh. It hit me when I realized that you never really confirmed that you were looking for Triana. In fact, all of your answers were intentionally vague and erratic. It's like you were playing some sort of game with us: answering the questions so that we *thought* this was about Triana, but never actually lying to us.

"And the more I turned this over in my head, the more I realized that, if it was about Tree, you would certainly have brought us in. But no. The only reason you would insist on doing this by yourself, the only reason you would risk the medical danger that you did, was because your guilt has driven you to seek some sort of connection to a dead girl that you feel you let down."

When he spoke, his voice was barely above a whisper. "I *did* let her down."

Lita sat back on the bench. "Okay, maybe you did. I know this is where I'm supposed to offer you pity and support and say something like, 'No, Bon, you did nothing wrong.' But I think on some level that, yes, you probably did let her down. She reached out to you because she thought you would help her navigate through the fear. And, in the process, she fell for you a bit. But, although you were drawn to the freaky parallels of your . . . your mutual oddities, let's say . . . you never shared the same feelings. And I think that has eaten at you since the day she died."

He turned to look back at her. "And what if it has? What business is it of yours? Like I told all of you, this is personal."

"Bon," Lita said, her voice growing tender. "Listen to me. I'm not condemning the fact that you didn't return Alexa's feelings. In fact, I've got a feeling that Triana is at the heart of that. If you let Alexa down—*if*, I'm saying—it might have been in the way you made her feel completely alone when she was sure she had someone who could walk her through her . . . uniqueness. You were, in her eyes, a kindred spirit, and yet you didn't always act that way."

He sat down in the soil, resting his back against the pump box, and clasped his arms around his knees. Lita watched him, her heart aching for him. She rose from the bench and walked over to him, settling onto the soil at his side.

"I'm not trying to make you feel bad," she said. "If anything, I'm trying to help. I'm trying to tell you that you shouldn't feel guilty about what happened; nobody could possibly have known what would happen with that vulture. Nobody."

"Alexa knew," Bon said.

"No. You said that she saw darkness, and she felt heaviness. And a strange feeling when she was around the vulture. But she didn't know that it would attack her."

Bon only shook his head.

"I understand how you feel," Lita said. "And I don't blame you for what you did with this." She held up the translator. "I just wish you had come to me, and confided in me. Alexa was my friend, too, you know."

She reached over to place a hand on his arm. "Did they tell you anything?"

Bon's head snapped around. "What?"

"Did the Cassini tell you anything?"

He peered into her eyes. "Are you serious? I thought you were angry about that."

"Of course I was angry. You should have come to me. We have no idea what these links will end up doing to you. But we do know that they're changing you."

"How?"

Lita removed her hand from his arm. "The scans that we ran on you are interesting. I compared them to the scans you had before the launch, along with the scans we made after the first contact back at Saturn. Your left cerebral hemisphere is undergoing some changes."

"Meaning . . . ?"

"Well, without getting too technical, two portions are expanding. One is called Wernicke's Area, the other Broca's Area. They both involve speech, whether it's language recognition or speech production. In other words, the Cassini are modifying your brain to allow you to communicate—and understand—their transmissions. Maybe even without needing the translator. At least that's my guess."

"So I really am becoming a freak," Bon said, shaking his head.

"I didn't say you were growing another head, it's just that the one you have is being remodeled. It's probably one of the reasons why Triana limited your access to the translator in the first place; she was just as worried as I am about all of the unknowns involved. And it's why you're certainly not connecting again without me around. Understand?"

He gazed back and forth between her eyes, attempting, it seemed, to read her thoughts. "Without you around. So . . . are you giving the translator back to me?"

"Tell me what you learned from the Cassini."

"Why?"

Lita drew lines in the soil. "Call it scientific curiosity."

He hesitated before responding. "I . . . I don't really know what they said. They tried to plant information into my head, but I passed out before anything substantial took hold."

"But you think they *were* answering your question?"

He nodded. "I think so."

She continued to scrape at the soil with her finger. "A line between this world, and the world of the hereafter . . ."

Bon gave her a curious look. "I don't believe this. You were furious at me for using the translator, and now you're . . . what? Becoming an accomplice?"

Lita smiled. "I told you, it's scientific curiosity."

He kept his gaze on her face, then suddenly raised his eyebrows. "Wait a minute," he said. "It's not just the science. You're talking to me about *my* guilt; but if the Cassini really are redesigning my brain, there's no way you'd let me connect again unless . . ."

Lita felt her heart rate pick up. "Unless what?"

Bon gave a slight nod. "Unless you're trying to deal with feelings of guilt yourself." When Lita didn't respond, he nodded again. "Of course. You've been beating yourself up over Alexa since the operation. You did nothing wrong then, and you did nothing wrong with the vulture, and yet—"

Lita cut him off by putting a hand over his mouth. "All right. That's enough."

His eyes were like lasers. He gently reached up and pulled her hand away. "As soon as you figured out what I've been doing, you didn't go to Gap or the Council. You came here, to talk with me. You *want* me to reach Alexa, don't you? Say what you want about the science, but you want to make sure she's okay, too. Somewhere. Somehow."

She was silent again, but in her mind she saw Manu's amulet hanging from the vidscreen. Faith. Fate. Science. Did any of those pieces fit together at all? Was she scrambling to *make* them fit, motivated by her own feelings of guilt? Was she being completely honest with Bon—and with herself—by claiming a purely scientific curiosity? The fact that she sidestepped the Council and came straight to Bon answered some of those questions.

She stood up and brushed the dirt off her pants. Slipping the translator back into her pocket, she said, "Let's keep this little discussion to ourselves for right now, okay? I'll talk with you about it later."

Bon could only stare up at her, scanning her face. Lita looked away, determined that he not see that her eyes had become wet.

Before either could say another word, their world erupted. A searing, blinding flash of light exploded through the clear panels of the dome. Lita and Bon both grunted in pain, clamping their eyes shut and throwing up hands to shield their faces. As quickly as it happened, it was gone.

22

The strain of it all eventually led Gap to one of the few places where he felt at home and at ease. Twenty minutes atop his Airboard gave him the opportunity to temporarily abandon any thoughts of the wormholes, the radiation crisis, the mystifying lightning flashes, the election, and Hannah. He cruised on his board, mere inches above the padded floor, riding the invisible force of gravity, feeling the ebb and flow of the attraction and adjusting his weight to steer. He kept his speed at an exhilarating level, but nowhere near his personal best. Today was not about setting records; it was about escape.

It was just after five o'clock. The voting window had closed two hours earlier, and Roc would be announcing the results at six. That should have dominated his thoughts, yet he couldn't take his mind off the conversation he'd had with Hannah. Suddenly the outcome of the Council Leader election took a backseat to her admission that she still cared for him. He grappled with whether or not he'd handled this news the right way. He'd simply responded that he felt the same way; should he have reached over and taken her into his arms?

Why did it have to be so hard?

After bantering with a few fellow die-hard Boarders in the bleachers—and thanking them for their hearty cries of good luck—Gap hefted his Airboard and trudged out of the room. As he made his way towards the lift on the lower level, he wondered whether it would be a good idea to stop by the Dining Hall after his shower, or whether it would be best to hear the news alone, in his room. If he won, it might be nice to be among fellow crew members. On the other hand, if he lost . . .

He came into view of the lift. At the same time he saw a figure, apparently having just stepped out of the lift, moving off in the opposite direction. He barely caught a glimpse before the person rounded the bend, heading down the corridor towards the Spider bay. But who would have business there? There were no maintenance assignments currently scheduled.

Curious, he tucked his Airboard under one arm and followed.

As he approached another turn, just before his favorite viewing window on the ship, he heard voices ahead. One voice in particular jumped out: Hannah's.

He crept up to the bend but stayed out of sight. There was no doubt that it was Hannah who was speaking.

"I don't care," she said. "I'm prepared for either result. In fact, I might actually feel relief if Gap wins."

The other person—presumably the figure Gap had seen walking away from the lift—gave only a low chuckle. It had a condescending ring to it.

"Laugh if you want," he heard Hannah say. "It shouldn't be news to you, not after all the times we've talked about this."

The moment he heard the reply, Gap froze. The voice was unmistakable.

"You have such a flair for being dramatic," Merit said. "Even when you're not trying to be. It must be the artistic side of you, the creative and rebellious gene that all artists seem to have. It doesn't change the fact that everything has gone exactly as we hoped so far. You easily won both of the forums, and the crew is behind you."

It was almost too much for Gap to handle. Merit? Merit was behind Hannah's run for office? He leaned against the wall, his heart slamming against his chest.

"The crew is behind Gap as well," Hannah said. "Regardless of the scare tactic you tried with that post—yes, I know it was you, don't give me that look. You're so confident about these election results, and I'm telling you right now that it could easily go either way."

"They loved your theory," Merit said.

"Sure. But it's another story when it comes to selecting someone to implement the ideas. Gap made great points, and his solution is just as viable as mine."

Gap wanted to run, run back to the lift, back to his room, seal himself inside and never come out. Instead, before he knew what he was doing, he pushed away from the wall and stepped around the bend.

Merit's back was to him. Hannah, however, looked over Merit's shoulder and saw Gap immediately. Her mouth dropped open. Merit, seeing the look, spun around. His face, too, registered surprise at first. But then, slowly, a defiant smirk took over.

"Gap . . ." Hannah said.

Gap felt the blood rush to his face. He let the Airboard slip to the floor, and his hands balled into fists at his side. "So . . . the two of you . . ."

Hannah stepped around Merit. "Gap, wait. I—"

"Don't bother," Gap said. "I couldn't believe it when you agreed to run for election, but now it all makes sense. You both had an ax to grind with me; what better way to get revenge, right? Team up to crush me."

"No, Gap, it's not like that."

"Really? Sure seems like it." Gap shook his head. "And to think I actually believed what you said to me a few hours ago."

"It's true."

"Save it."

Merit laughed. "What are you so worked up about, Gap? You should just pick up your toy there and go back to the track. We have things to work out." He gently placed a hand on Hannah's shoulder. "Don't we, babe?"

Gap felt an instant flash of rage. He began to take a step toward Merit, but stopped himself. He felt the muscles in his arms stiffen, and his jaw clenched together.

Hannah spun to face Merit, shoving his hand aside. "Get your hands off me, Merit! Do you hear me? And shut your mouth!"

"No, let him talk," Gap said. "I guess it was his idea all along to have you run. He's the one who nominated you, right, *babe*? You two are a beautiful couple."

Merit only laughed again.

Hannah turned back to Gap. "You've got to believe me, we are not a couple. He's just saying that to get back at you, to hurt you. Don't you understand? It's not like that at all."

"Oh, really?"

"I meant what I told you. This . . . this isn't . . ." She stopped and let out a long breath.

Gap shook his head again. "I'll leave you two alone."

"Gap, no . . ."

He had barely started to turn, and out of the corner of his eye could see Hannah reaching for him, when suddenly a violent bang rocked the ship. Gap and Hannah were thrown against the far wall, slamming into it with enough force that it knocked the wind out of them. Merit landed in a pile a few feet away, crumpling to the floor at a bad angle, and Gap heard the snap of a bone.

All of the lights went out, and they were plunged into absolute darkness.

23

If he'd blacked out, Gap figured it couldn't have been for more than a few seconds. He tried to roll over, but Hannah was sprawled across his legs. He could hear her groan and begin to stir, and after a few moments she sat up. He rolled into a sitting position and took stock of his condition.

A lump was already bulging on his forehead, and he could taste blood from undoubtedly biting his lip. His right wrist ached from bracing for the impact with the wall. On top of that he felt slightly nauseated, but that appeared to be the extent of his wounds.

He began to fumble with his hands to locate Hannah when the lights flicked back on at what seemed half power. Hannah sat against the wall, a small trail of blood stretching from beside her right eye to just below the jawline. She was grasping her right elbow and wincing. She blinked to adjust to the light, then looked over at Gap with wide eyes.

"Was that . . . what I think it was?" she said.

Gap didn't answer. He stood up gingerly, wringing his hand to work the kinks out of his wrist, then looked over at Merit, who was lying facedown, his arm twisted unnaturally beneath him. He wasn't moving.

Gap heard Hannah say something about getting help, then she was gone, limping around the bend to the nearest intercom. He knelt beside the fallen figure and saw that Merit was breathing but unconscious. There was no visible blood. Until trained medical help arrived, Gap thought it unwise to move him.

He was anxious to get up to the Control Room and was grateful when Hannah hurried back.

"Manu said they're swamped with calls right now," she told him. "He said someone will be down in just a few minutes."

"I've gotta go," Gap said. "Stay here until they arrive, and check in with me later." He threw a quick glance down at Merit, and then back to Hannah. Her face had a pleading look.

"Gap, believe me—"

He cut her off. "We can talk later." Without another word he turned and rushed towards the lift.

Ascending to the top level, he summoned the ship's computer. "Roc, do you have a damage report yet?"

"Just filtering everything now. The radiation shield dropped again, as you might expect, and when it stayed down for five seconds I automatically diverted power from the ion drive, as you proposed. It seems to have done the trick . . . for now. The shield is back up, but I can't promise for how long."

Gap burst out of the lift on *Galahad*'s upper level and immediately saw crew members assisting others towards Sick House. Most of the injured were either cradling an arm or holding a compress of sorts over a bleeding wound. None appeared too serious, but Gap wondered what the final casualty list would look like.

The Control Room buzzed with activity. Gap logged into his

Engineering work station and surveyed the data. As he did so, the ship's lights came back to full power.

"Shield still holding?" he asked Roc.

"Yes," the computer said. "I took it upon myself to clip one percent of power from the drive. I'm sure you understand the significance of that amount."

Despite the nausea, Gap managed a thin smile. During the initial encounter with the Cassini, the alien presence had attempted to "improve" the starship that was rocketing through their neighborhood by boosting the ion drive. Although their intentions were good, the ship's engines were not designed to handle the stress, and ultimately the maneuver came dangerously close to destroying the ship. In the end, Bon was able to communicate with the Cassini and prevent the disaster. And yet, for reasons unknown, the ship managed to escape with a fractional increase in power.

"Our little one-percent gift from the Cassini," Gap muttered. "Knowing how much you care about them, I'm sure it pained you to siphon that away."

"If your sarcastic comment is meant to imply that I somehow derive joy by regifting their contribution, nothing could be further from the truth. It merely seemed a practical solution."

"Uh-huh," Gap said. "I have to say, Roc, your snippy attitude about the Cassini is quite immature."

"Me? Immature?" Roc said. "You can't see it, but I'm virtually sticking my tongue out at you. Back to business: other than the shield, the ship's primary systems check out okay; Lita and Manu are treating approximately twenty crew members so far in Sick House, mostly scrapes and bruises; and the lump on your forehead gives you a somewhat Quasimodo-like appearance. Very rugged looking, something you normally don't pull off too well."

Gap lightly brushed his forehead with his fingers, then cringed. "Well, obviously we need to talk about the shock wave. Probably no big mystery about what caused that. Would I be correct in assuming that we are now graced with the opening of another wormhole nearby?"

"Much closer, in fact, than the others we experienced," Roc said. "That explains the extremely violent concussion. Almost like it was tracking us through space better than last time, and placed itself in the perfect position to intercept us. A perfect pass, you might say."

"What's your calculation for contact?"

Roc paused for a few seconds, then said: "One hour, four minutes. However, assuming Hannah's theory is correct, we should experience a few of those delightful shock waves before that."

Gap pulled his chair over and sat down. The nausea had subsided, but his head and wrist still throbbed. He looked up and nodded appreciation when one of the Control Room personnel handed him a cup of water.

His mind scrambled through the information Roc had provided. If another wormhole had ripped through the fabric of space, and with pinpoint accuracy in order to intercept the ship, it was quite obviously there for a reason. Could it be an attack on *Galahad*? Were the beings responsible for the vultures out to avenge their fallen soldier, perhaps by launching a fleet of the ominous dark creatures?

Or would the vultures' caretakers be arriving to personally take matters into their own hands?

The next five minutes were spent diagnosing the rejuvenated radiation shield, the effect of the ion drive power shift, and the expanding injury update from Sick House. Lita reported that the toll had climbed to twenty-nine.

"Lots of bumps and bruises," she said over the intercom. "Four people are going to be admitted to the hospital ward for a bit, though."

Gap paused, staring at the console. "Uh . . . does that include Merit?"

"It does," Lita said. "His arm is broken, and he cracked a couple of ribs. I'm about to run a scan for any internal damage."

Gap felt his emotions twist. Less than an hour earlier it had taken everything in his power to keep from lashing out at Merit. What did it say about his character, he wondered, that news of Merit's injuries caused him to feel a twinge of satisfaction? Did that make him a monster?

And if he felt those sinister feelings for Merit, why did he not feel the same way about Hannah? She had deceived him, and she had teamed up with Merit Simms. Merit Simms! Shouldn't he, after all, have the same dark thoughts about her?

But he didn't. Despite the blow to his heart, he knew that he still cared about her. What did it all mean?

He decided that it was not the time for a self-inspection of his soul. "What about Hannah?" he said to Lita. "She had some blood—"

"She's fine. Might have a tiny scar to remember it all by, but otherwise she's okay. Let's talk about you."

"I'm okay," Gap said.

"That's not what I heard. Hannah said that you slammed your extremely thick skull into the wall. Well, she said your head; I added the thick part. When can you stop in to let us at least check you out?"

Gap again dabbed at the lump. "I'm all right. Besides, we've got another wormhole coming up fast. I can't leave right now."

"I knew you'd say that," Lita said. "Manu should be walking in your door any second. Don't be stubborn, let him spend three minutes looking at you."

"I didn't know you guys made house calls," Gap said. "Let me know how things are going later." He ended the conversation as the door slid open, admitting Manu. True to Lita's estimate, it took only a few minutes to pronounce Gap fit for duty.

"You'll be sore for a day or two," Manu said. "If you feel the need for a pain pill, let me know." He gave Gap a wry smile. "In the meantime, you kinda look like that hunchback character. What's his name? Quasimodo?"

"Ha ha ha!" Roc blurted from the speaker. "Do I know my classic literature, or what? Ring the bell, Gap, ring the bell!"

Gap shook his head and thanked Manu. "If I need a pill, it will be because of a completely separate headache."

"Unappreciated, that's what I am," the computer said. "Steering the conversation back to the tiny matter at hand, namely our humble ship galloping towards a gaping gash in the universe . . ."

"Yes?"

"We're about fifty-two minutes out. I've nudged the ship so that we'll cruise past the opening rather than down the hatch. Even so, it's much closer than before, and even with my dazzling intellect it'll be hard to predict what effect that will have on the ship. If Hannah's bruise theory is correct—and this will be a good test—we're in for a bumpy ride."

Gap imagined a water skier, bouncing over the wake of a boat, riding out the turbulence.

"Can you nudge us outward a little more, please?" he said. "Let's try to give ourselves the biggest cushion we can." He dropped back into his chair and began to calculate just how close they would be coming to the wormhole.

He realized that six o'clock had slipped past. The election results should have been announced by this point, but Roc, it seemed, had shuffled that bit of business down several notches. Gap was thankful; after what he'd stumbled across on the lower level, he couldn't stand the idea that the team of Hannah and Merit might have defeated him. He opened his mouth to suggest that Roc hold the results until this latest emergency was over and done with, but held off. That was a decision for the entire Council.

Focus, he told himself. He bent back over the console and directed his energies to a new area: the radiation shield. If *Galahad* was minutes away from a furious storm, it might be time to divert even more energy to the shield.

As if on cue, the ship's lights dimmed again, and within seconds a call came from Engineering. It was Julya.

"Let me guess," Gap said. "What's the status of the shield right now?"

"Well," she said, "stable, I suppose. It dropped out for just over a second, then came back, then out for another second."

"Roc," Gap said, "I think it's time for one of those executive decisions. Let's drop another two percent into the shield. Can it handle that input?"

"If not, we'll return it to the manufacturer with a very stern letter. Should take about three minutes." The computer paused, and then added, "Uh-oh."

Gap recognized the tone. Roc had only shifted to that tone on a few occasions, and it had always preceded bad news.

"The space around us has just become a bit more congested," Roc said.

"Explain," Gap said.

"We know that the wormholes are not used for decoration; they're passageways. And it seems that a few things have spilled out of this passageway, right into our path."

A knot instantly materialized in Gap's stomach, and he felt an icy streak race through his veins. "How many things are we talking about?"

"Lots," Roc said. "As in . . ." After a few seconds delay, he added, "Roughly two thousand."

Gap not only felt a stab of fear himself, he swore that he could feel the collective fear roiling through the atmosphere of the Control Room as each crew member absorbed the news. Two *thousand*? His mind conjured up images of a vast squadron of pitch-black vultures, circling ahead, waiting to intercept and latch on to *Galahad*. He imagined that each person in the room had painted a similar picture.

He brought himself upright in his chair and injected as much composure into his voice as possible. He was still the commander of the ship. "Do you have enough data yet to determine the size and trajectory?"

"Scanning again," Roc said. "No doubt that all but one of them are vultures."

Gap gazed up at the room's giant vidscreen, but saw only the blazing star field. "All but one?"

"Well, isn't this interesting," the computer said.

"Roc, tell me!"

"It would seem that we might be getting some of our property back. Besides the nasty critters, that's our pod that just popped out of the wormhole. It's back."

24

The door to the Conference Room slid open and Lita rushed in. The other Council members were seated around the table, waiting for her. She had turned things over to Manu and the rest of the Sick House staff in order to squeeze in a few minutes for the emergency meeting. Gap began talking before she even took her seat.

"As you probably heard, or at least guessed, another wormhole has exploded onto the scene. This one seems to have practically tracked us. The ripple effect has once again struck our shields, and I've had Roc divert some power from the ion drive engines in order to provide us with at least a little more protection for the time being.

"At our current speed we should fly past the opening of the wormhole in about thirty-six minutes. However, before we reach that point we'll come across a squadron of vultures which popped out and are now gradually plotting an intercept course to us. And this time there's a lot of them. A couple thousand."

Gap could see Channy visibly shiver. Lita's face went pale;

he'd known that the healing she'd been working on since Alexa's death would take a hit with this news, and he felt for her.

"But there's more," he said, hoping to quickly divert the focus away from the sinister-looking vultures. "The pod is back."

All three of his fellow Council members reacted at once. Lita let out a gasp; Channy's eyes went wide and she threw both hands up around her face.

Bon's mouth dropped open and he gripped the edge of the table with both hands. Gap had never seen the Swede react so dramatically to anything during their voyage. He stared down the table at Bon, trying to read what was spinning inside his head. Recovering at once, Bon stood and walked over to the water dispenser, keeping his back to Gap.

"So she's back," Channy said, breaking the spell.

"The *pod* is back," Gap said. "As for what's inside, we have no idea. We've tried making radio contact, but there's been no response. I'm hopeful, of course, but unless we can get inside to look around . . ." He let his voice trail off.

Lita was staring at Bon's back. She said, "Do we have any ideas on how these . . . wormhole people, whoever they might be, were able to find us?"

Gap shook his head. "Before, we figured that the vultures were communicating with them, giving them coordinates. Now, with no vultures around—at least none that we know of—we have no idea. But Roc has a theory that might clear up at least one mystery we've been dealing with. Roc, wanna share what you told me?"

"The first thing I told Gap," the computer said, "was to let someone help him color coordinate his clothes. After that we got down to business about this new wormhole, and the question of how they knew where to find us. Specifically, the flashes of light."

Lita said nothing and kept her head lowered, staring at the table. Bon had walked slowly back to the table and, for a change, seemed very interested in a Council discussion.

"Wait," Channy said. "They found us . . . with light?"

Roc said, "They found us using a method not unlike the way old-style computer programmers worked. The light was more than just light; it was a ping."

Channy sighed. "I'm going to need some special tutoring on this."

"At your service. In the early days of computers—long before you had such magnificent creations like me—computer techs would test connections between computers, or between computers and websites, by sending out what was known as a ping. They could identify an IP address and gauge the delay between the signal's origination and its receipt. What the wormhole masters were doing, it would seem, is not much different; they were sending interstellar pings to locate us."

Since Gap, Lita, and Bon remained silent, Channy spoke up again. "But how would they know where to even send this ping?"

"Still working on that," Roc said. "But I can say, with strong confidence, that we've found yet another way that these creatures manipulate dark energy. Those mystery particles within the light flashes? I'm pretty sure that's what they are. And if I'm right—and I usually am—they're somehow able to send their dark energy pings across vast distances. Perhaps even infinite distances."

The room was silent for a moment. Then Gap sat forward and said, "I would love to spend more time puzzling out their methods, but it's not our most important issue right now. Before we worry about how they've found us, we need to concentrate on capturing the pod and getting it back into the Spider bay." He glanced around the table. The last time they'd gone fishing for this same pod, some had questioned the wisdom of bringing it aboard. "I'm assuming that there's no argument about doing that, right?"

Channy shook her head. Bon remained still. A thoughtful look crossed Lita's face, and she said, "Of course we need to bring it aboard. But Manu brought up a good point. We have no idea where the pod has been, or what it might be carrying. I'm strongly suggesting that we quarantine the bay, and anyone near the pod should wear protective gear until we determine whether there's any contamination."

Gap nodded. "All right. I appreciate that." He looked at each of the Council members. "What concerns me right now is that the pod is surrounded by two thousand vultures, like fighter planes escorting a bomber. I doubt that any of them will fly into the open Spider bay door when the time comes. We saw what happens when they encounter oxygen, so I expect them to keep their distance. But it's still a little daunting to have that many buzzing around us."

Channy spoke up. "And how do we know there aren't more waiting to fly out of the wormhole? Or . . . something else that might pop out?"

"We don't know," Gap said. "I just wanted to make sure that everyone was up to speed on what was happening. I want us to be very careful about all of this, because we have to go under the assumption that Triana might still be aboard the pod."

There was silence for a moment before Lita said, "I take it that the election results are temporarily being withheld?"

Gap turned one hand palm up. "That's up to the three of you."

Looks were exchanged. Lita seemed to go into deep thought

before she spoke again. "Given several of the circumstances, I think it would be best to wait. I know it's only a possibility, but if Triana is really aboard the pod—and assuming that she's okay—it wouldn't make much sense to release an announcement right now. Delaying the results a few hours won't make much difference anyway, will it?"

Gap looked around at the other Council members. He was the only one who knew about Merit's involvement with Hannah's election bid. That meant that the one person most likely to squawk about a delay was lying incapacitated in the Clinic.

"I don't think it matters," Channy said. "I vote to see if Triana is back or not."

Although a majority had spoken, all eyes turned to Bon. He shrugged and said, "Sure."

Gap felt a sense of relief. He couldn't deny that the election results weighed heavily upon him, and the distraction caused by the pod's return—not to mention the vultures—at least temporarily shelved that issue. Now, more than ever, he yearned for Triana to reappear.

"Okay," he said to the Council. "We'll postpone the announcement of the election results until we see what develops in the next twelve to twenty-four hours."

"But I know who won!" Roc said with an impish tone. "How do you expect me to keep a secret like that?"

"Nobody understands that better than me," Channy said. "You can tell me later in private. I won't breathe a word to anyone."

Gap rolled his eyes. "On that note, this meeting is adjourned. Channy, will you please find Hannah and let her know our decision? I'd prefer that someone tell her in person, rather than through e-mail or the intercom." He excused himself and quickly left the room. Channy waved good-bye to the others and followed him into the corridor.

As Bon walked towards the door, Lita reached out and grasped his arm. The door closed, leaving them alone in the Conference Room. He looked down at her hand, and then into her dark eyes. "Yes?" he said.

Lita propped herself against the table. "You realize what happened, right?"

"I don't know what you mean," he said.

"You don't really think this new wormhole opened up right in front of us by chance, do you?"

Bon crossed his arms. "How would I know?"

"It's not by chance," Lita said. "I told Channy a while ago that we needed to become some sort of lighthouse for Triana to find her way back to us. We needed a beacon."

"And?"

"And that beacon was you."

He stared at her. "I still don't know what you mean."

"I think you do."

He seemed to process for a moment, then said, "If you're suggesting that I did this with the translator—"

Lita nodded. "I know what you're going to say: you made contact with the Cassini hoping to find some way to reach Alexa. But in the process you apparently sent out some kind of signal, or beacon, that these . . . these beings, or creatures, or whatever they are, were able to home in on."

"You don't know that," he said.

"Of course I don't *know* it," Lita said. "But it's the only thing that makes sense. You reached out, and they grabbed on. Those . . . those pings that Roc mentioned. They had to have something to guide their search. And except for the very last flash—which was probably just a last-minute check to make sure we were where they thought we'd be—the first two flashes happened right after your connections." She paused and gave Bon a smile. "Am I right?"

When Bon didn't answer, she continued. "Listen, I don't know if we owe this to fate, or to the workings of a higher power in the universe. But you went looking for Alexa, and as a result you might have led Triana back home."

Bon pressed his lips together. Neither said a word for what seemed a long time.

"And another thing," Lita said. "This helps to satisfy my scientific curiosity that you shrugged off. Specifically the power of thought."

"That's just a theory," Bon said. "It's never been proven."

"I think you just did."

He shook his head and gave a harsh laugh. "You put an awful lot of stock in my redesigned brain."

Lita pushed off from the table and faced him. "I put a lot of stock in the power of the human mind, yes. But I'm not thinking about your mind by itself. I've seen studies that show what large groups of people can do when they focus together on something. Seems to me that putting the power of the Cassini behind your thoughts could accomplish things we might never have believed possible. Like reaching through space to find Triana. And if it can do that . . ."

Her voice trailed off, and again they stared at one another. When she spoke again, it was barely above a whisper.

"If science can explain how you're able to reach across a galaxy to draw someone home, I don't see why it can't reach across other voids as well."

She could see Bon swallow hard. Finally, he took a deep breath and said, "Maybe. Or maybe we're both crazy. Did you consider that scientific possibility, too?" With that, he turned and walked out of the Conference Room.

Lita watched him leave. Her hand reached up to her neck, to the charcoal-colored stone that hung from the silver strand. Her gaze shifted to the window, and she considered the brilliant display of stars, and what might lie beyond them.

25

Gap delegated several of his responsibilities to various team members in the Control Room, then called down to Engineering. Ruben reported that the shield was stable for the time being, but that he would stay on top of the situation and report any changes immediately.

Roc had spent the past half hour plotting the maneuvers that would be necessary to capture the pod and bring it safely into the Spider bay. Gap reviewed the details and the timetable, and decided to oversee the action from the bay's control room. With about ten minutes to go, he donned the pressurized EVA suit per Manu's recommendation and stepped into the glass-enclosed booth that looked out over *Galahad*'s vast hangar.

Built to hold the ship's maintenance and transport vehicles, nicknamed Spiders because of their shape and multiple hinged arms that radiated from their shell, the room was a giant airlock that emptied into space. They had launched with ten of the small craft, only eight of which were capable of sustaining life-support systems, and one of those was lost during the showdown with the stowaway. That left *Galahad* with seven fully functioning transport vehicles once they reached Eos, a dilemma that had been pushed to the back burner for the time being.

The bay had also housed the metallic pod which had originally been launched from the doomed space station orbiting Titan, and which ultimately carried Triana through the alien wormhole. If all went according to plan, that pod would be safely tucked back into the bay within the next half hour.

Gap fought to repress the usual tinge of discomfort he felt whenever he stood in the Spider bay's control room. He would always associate this site with heartbreak, for it was in this room that he had witnessed a connection between Triana and Bon. True, it had lasted only a few seconds, but it was an image that he knew he would never be able to erase. For the moment, however, he had work to do, and ironically that work involved rescuing Triana.

Assuming she was on the pod. "Please," he said quietly to himself, "let her be there. Please."

"Roc," he said. "Is the pod maneuvering under its own power?"

"No, it appears to be drifting. My guess would be that it's being dangled out there like a piece of cheese for us to pick up, and, should we decide to take a sniff and pass it by, they would be able to gather it back up and stuff it back through the wormhole."

That made sense to Gap. He pulled up the data on the control room's vidscreen and watched the numbers counting down. "Let's make it clear to them that we have every intention of retrieving the pod. If the bay is clear, go ahead and open the door, please."

A minute later he watched through the window as one of the bay's large doors silently slid open.

"Magnetic beam is ready," Roc said. "Contact in approximately three minutes." He paused for a moment, then added, "Apparently opening the bay door was like sending up a flare. Our little vulture friends are now making a beeline for us."

Gap shifted his gaze from the vidscreen to the bay's open door, and an instinctual shudder passed through him. Even though the oxygen-laced atmosphere of the ship would prevent the part-mechanical-part-biological creatures from operating inside *Galahad*, he couldn't help but feel that he had made the ship vulnerable by simply propping open the door. A chilling vision of waves of vultures, soaring through the opening, flashed before his eyes. He pushed it aside and concentrated on the pod.

"One minute to pod capture," Roc said. "P.S., the escorts have arrived and are circling the ship. Correction, all but one are circling. That one has latched on to us, not far from the open door."

"Can you give me a camera shot?" Gap said.

"It should be up on your vidscreen any moment."

There was a flicker on the screen, and then it appeared. Gap recoiled as the image came into focus.

The dark black vulture stood out against the gray exterior of *Galahad* like a cosmic wound. Triangular in shape, it was pressed against the ship by an unseen force, a force that the crew now assumed was related to the mysterious dark energy that saturated the universe.

On the vidscreen he could see the vulture's wings, now folded up along its sides, and with some magnification he was able to make out its rough, pebbled surface. The vents which ran like stitches along the sides were pulsing open and closed, and by adjusting the camera angle Gap could pick out a faint blue-green glow seeping from underneath. Though no wider than two feet across, the vulture presented an imposing—and intimidating—aura.

Gap's dark thoughts were interrupted by Roc. "Twenty seconds. Beginning power-up . . . now."

The vidscreen switched back to a graphical display, and Gap watched the pod's capture unfold. A magnetic beam, capable of grasping nearby objects and tugging them into the *Spider* bay, was about to be utilized for the second time since they had departed Earth, and both occasions involved the same small metal craft.

Icons that represented both *Galahad* and the pod appeared to slip past each other. Then the pod's image momentarily froze before slowly reversing course and tracking towards the ship. At the same time, Roc announced, "Capture complete. I'm now reeling her in like a marlin."

Gap let out a long breath. "Great job. Will you let the other Council members know the status, please?" He thought about it for a second, then added, "And let Hannah know, too. Thanks."

For all he knew, Hannah was the acting Council Leader of *Galahad*, even if nobody knew it yet.

He found himself fidgeting for the next few minutes as the pod crept along the magnetic stream towards the rendezvous. Four crew members, each wearing the necessary EVA suit, entered the control room. Gap nodded at them, then quickly updated them on the situation. He noticed, without commenting, that one of the crew members held an oxygen gun at his side.

A reminder, Gap thought, *that we have to do everything we can to protect ourselves, especially if we're up against a formidable opponent.* Hopefully it wouldn't be necessary.

"Stand by, I'll have the fish in the boat in about one minute," Roc said. "I'm a little disappointed this one didn't kick and fight like the others usually do. Might have to throw it back."

The door to the hallway opened and Channy walked in. Her eyes were wide, and for one of the few times on the voyage she was speechless. She gave a small wave to Gap, then walked over to the window.

Seconds later the starlight pouring through the open bay door was blotted out. The pod hovered just outside, and then gradually floated into the vast hangar. It set down in the same spot it had occupied before Triana's departure, and the bay door was once again sealed.

Thankfully, Gap noted that not a single vulture had flown into the ship. It appeared that they were content to simply escort the pod back home. Content, at least, for the moment.

"Pressurizing," Roc said.

Lita entered the room out of breath. "Well?" she said, then put her face up to the glass. "So . . . nothing else got in?"

Gap shook his head. "No. One of them is stuck on the ship right outside the bay, and the others are orbiting us like electrons."

He turned to the crew members who stood ready. "We'll go in as soon as the pressurization is complete. The first order of business: I want a complete visual scan of the pod. Top, bottom, sides, everywhere. I want to know if there's anything attached, anything at all."

Addressing Lita and Channy, he said, "I'm going in with the recovery unit, but I'd rather not take too many chances with the rest of the Council. It's not wise for all of us to be in there at the same time, not until everything checks out." He saw the disappointment on their faces, and quickly added, "I know you want to go in, but for now it's best if you wait here. Lita, I'll need you standing by in case of an emergency."

"I brought my little black bag," she said, patting the satchel that hung from her shoulder.

Gap nodded. "Roc, let's get a complete external scan for radiation before I open this door, please."

"Already underway," the computer said. "Early indications are normal."

Just as they were preparing to enter the bay, the door to the hallway opened again. Gap assumed it might be additional crew members coming to help and looked back over his shoulder with a casual glance.

It was Bon.

He stood in the doorway, in full EVA attire, holding his helmet under one arm. Lita and Channy were glued to the window and hadn't noticed. Gap and Bon stared at each other for a moment in an awkward wordless exchange.

Bon never showed up unless specifically instructed to do so, Gap thought. He even treated each scheduled Council meeting like a major imposition in his busy life. And now he was here?

Lita finally turned. She looked back and forth between Gap and Bon, then walked over to stand next to the Swede. "Hey, I'm glad you're here." She glanced up at Gap and said, "Maybe it would be a good idea for Bon to go with you. Just in case."

Gap watched the two of them intently. Something had passed between them, a silent look of understanding. He turned back to the door without a word; he didn't want Bon to go with him, but could think of no reasonable argument to keep him out. It wasn't worth the time it would take to thrash it out. Instead, he punched in the code to break the airlock and led the small party of crew members into the hangar. He kept his gaze on the gleaming metal pod resting straight ahead, but his mind couldn't help but replay the earlier scene between Bon and Triana. It shook him, and he clenched his hands into fists as he walked.

Soon the party had fanned out around the pod, although Bon chose to hang back, simply staring at it. A quick examination revealed nothing out of the ordinary; the craft looked exactly as it had the first time it had been brought aboard. Two windows dotted the front end of the small vessel, while block lettering and flag emblems on one side identified the countries of Earth originally responsible for its mission.

Gap walked to the rear hatch of the pod and stopped, facing the external emergency panel. He remembered their first encounter with this particular vessel, how Triana had stood in this exact spot while he watched nearby, his arm in a sling. Lita had been the first to board that time; today, nothing would stop him from being the first inside.

He had memorized the necessary code, and now punched the keys to open a small access panel. When it flipped open with a hiss, he flexed his fingers and reached inside to another keypad. After entering another string of numbers, he grasped the small handle inside the panel and looked back towards the window of the control booth. Lita gave him a supportive smile and a thumbs up.

He pulled the handle. A puff of air brushed against his helmet, and, with a metallic sigh, the hatch popped open a few inches.

Unlike their first foray into the pod, when it had loomed dark and lifeless, this time the interior was bathed in routine operating lights. They flickered, as if barely holding on to power. Not as spooky as before, Gap thought. Taking a deep breath, he reached up to the handrail in order to pull himself inside.

Without warning, his arm was grasped in a firm grip. With a start, he turned to look into a pair of ice-blue eyes.

"I'll go," Bon said, inches away from his face.

Gap was frozen for a moment, then collected himself and

shook Bon's hand away. "What are you talking about?"

"I'll go," Bon said again.

"What's gotten into you?" Gap said.

Bon's eyes bore into him, but he said nothing. Gap shook his head and uttered a sarcastic chuckle.

"I appreciate the offer, Bon, but I can handle it this time." Without waiting for a reply, Gap pushed him aside and grabbed the handrail. He pulled himself up into the pod's open hatch and stepped inside. He immediately felt Bon clamber up behind him.

The interior was different. The passenger seats which once occupied space in the back were missing, and the suspended-animation tubes had been disconnected and shoved to one side. Gap took a moment to orient himself to the changes, then looked towards the forward end of the ship. Two seats in the cockpit area were silhouetted against the glow of the instrument panel.

From behind, he saw a head tilted to one side in the pilot's seat and a cascade of dark hair. An arm hung limply, fingers curled up against the floor. Gap rushed forward and knelt beside the figure in the chair.

His heart pounded as he stared into Triana's face.

Her eyes were only half open, a ghastly look that immediately made Gap fear the worst. He leaned forward and felt a surge of relief that she was breathing. Looking up, he saw Bon kneeling on the other side of Triana. He was concentrating on her with an intensity that Gap had never seen in him before, at least not outside of his work. Mixed in with the intensity was a look of . . .

Gap realized that it was a look of tenderness. He suddenly felt certain that if he hadn't been there, Bon would have brushed her face with his hand.

Bon's expression changed as soon as he met Gap's gaze, and

he leveled an almost defiant look. Neither spoke for a few seconds, and in that instant Gap wondered if he had completely misread Bon from the beginning. He was cold, he was rebellious, he was uncooperative, he was aggravating.

But he was here. He *did* care. And, Gap thought, it must be killing him to show it.

"Listen," Gap said. "Go back to the booth and send Lita in here. We need to get Triana to Sick House right now." He paused, and then added, "Please."

With another quick glance down at Triana's face, then a curt nod, Bon disappeared. Seconds later Gap could hear the recovery unit members scrambling up into the pod, but he kept his attention on Tree. He gently straightened her in the chair and deposited her hands in her lap. Then he did what he swore Bon was on the verge of doing: his gloved fingers brushed across her forehead, pulling the hair out of her face.

Lita soon joined him. "Help is coming," she said. "Don't worry, we'll take care of her."

"I know," Gap said, and felt himself on the verge of tears. Not very leaderlike, he decided, and stood up to examine what was going on in the back of the pod. The others were gathered in a knot, deep in conversation about something.

Suddenly one of the crew members turned to him, a look of either shock or horror on her face; he couldn't decide which. "What is it?" he said, walking back to join the group.

She gulped. "Triana brought something back with her."

She and the others stood aside as Gap approached. In the odd flickering light, he saw what appeared to be an aquarium.

Floating inside was the last thing Gap expected to see in outer space.

S omething tells me that this time it's not a cat.

   Okay, just so I have all of this straight, let's go over what we've learned, shall we? The ship is streaking across the intergalactic void at a ridiculous speed, but is bouncing over cosmic speed bumps caused by a rupture in space from a wormhole that some unknown alien society has seen fit to throw in our faces. At the same time, these bumps and bruises are slowly but methodically tearing apart the atomic structure of the space around us and, eventually, the space within us, if we don't do something soon.

   We've witnessed something that the crew is calling space lightning, but would seem to be a tracking system that's somehow tied into Bon's newly altered brain.

   Then, on top of that, we have vultures who have once again descended upon our happy vessel and are currently circling us like . . . well, like vultures.

   And Merit Simms is back on the scene.

   Wait, there's more. Hannah and Gap can't seem to figure things out between them, and Bon is somehow standing on the corner at the intersection of Love and Loneliness. If our brooding farmer isn't careful, he's going to step off the curb and get run over by the Regret Express.

There is some good news, however. Triana, bless her soul, is back. Yes, we're all happy, and I'm sure there will be cake in the Rec Room, but I think we also agree that the girl has some explaining to do.

When she's able to talk, of course, but still . . .

And then there's the matter of this aquarium thing, or whatever it is, and the special guest inside. Are we finally going to meet the makers of the creepy vultures? Are we going to learn the secrets of the wormholes? Will we ever know exactly why Gap's hair stands straight up, even when he first climbs out of bed in the morning? How does it do that?

No whining from you about all of these questions, okay? Let's just keep riding along with our gallant star travelers and see what develops. Besides, you've got it easy; I'm the one who has to carry around the secret of the election and not say a peep.

I'll meet you back here for volume number six.

The Galahad Legacy

Her eyes fluttered open for a brief second, but the light seemed harsh, making her reluctant to open them again. The last thing she remembered was sitting in the cockpit of the pod, her heart racing as she again spiraled down into the wormhole. Her first experience doing that had taught her that it would not be pleasant.

But now she was lying on a bed, a sheet up to her neck, while muffled voices floated in from nearby. Her curiosity finally won out and she chanced another glimpse, cracking her eyes, allowing them to acclimate as she determined her surroundings. Of course it had to be *Galahad*, her mind told her, but her experiences in the past week—was it a week? was it a year?—kept her from accepting anything until she could see it with her own eyes.

Although, she had to admit, what she'd recently seen with those eyes was mind-shattering.

She pried her lids open a bit wider. When the room gradually swam into focus, she positively identified it as the hospital ward on the ship. She let out a contented sigh.

The sound must have alerted the people in the room, because moments later a shape loomed over her. Pulling her gaze upward, she felt a wave of comfort when the face of Lita Marques beamed at her.

"Welcome home, Tree," Lita said. "Why don't you stick around for a while?"

Triana Martell found the strength to smile, and mumbled a thick "hi."

"I'm sure you have questions galore," Lita said. "Let me answer a few before you ask. Yes, you're back safely; at least my preliminary scan doesn't show any physical problems, unless you have any aches you want to share with me." When Triana shook her head once, Lita continued. "Everyone here is fine, not counting the usual drama and a few bumps and bruises. The ship itself has a few problems, but Gap can get you caught up with that. And, let's see . . ."

She sat on the edge of the bed. "Lots of people have come by to welcome you back, but I've shooed them away for now. Oh, and the friend you brought with you is doing okay. Well, at least as far as I can tell."

Triana stared up at Lita, then cleared her throat and croaked, "Where?"

Lita nodded towards the door. "Down the hall. Same place we had the vulture. Only this time we're keeping people out. Remember, it was a zoo when we brought in the vulture. I get the feeling that this is much different, so we're keeping a lid on things for now." She paused and studied Triana's face. "It's actually quite different, isn't it?"

Rising up on her elbows, Triana looked at the table beside her. "Is that water?"

Lita helped her take a few sips. "No comment about . . . it?"

Triana licked her lips, then rubbed her eyes. "I'll have plenty of comments for all of you." She swallowed more water and felt her strength returning. "You're not gonna keep me in bed just because I passed out, are you?"

"Like I said, you seem fine," Lita said, standing up. "You know me, I'll always caution against doing too much after a traumatic experience, or a shock to the system. I'm guessing you've had both. But I know these are special circumstances, too. Let's get some food and water in you, we'll watch you for an hour or so, and then you can walk out of here. Deal?"

Triana lay back and smiled at her friend. "I won't fight you on that. I'm starving."

Lita patted her on the leg. "Good to hear. We'll get you something right away. Time to feed all of my patients anyway."

"All?" Triana said.

"Uh-huh. That wormhole you rode in on has banged up a few people. In fact . . ." Lita lowered her voice. "Your good friend Merit Simms is just three beds down. Sleeping, thanks to pain medication. You'll probably be gone before he wakes up."

She walked towards the door. "Don't wander off, or we'll bring you back and put you in the bed next to him."

Gap Lee trudged along *Galahad*'s curved hallway toward his room. It was well after midnight, and the halls were deserted. Exhausted, he wondered when he'd be able to crash for a good ten or twelve hours. With Triana's return, and the surprise which accompanied her, it might not be anytime soon.

He tried to wrap his brain around that surprise. Tucked into the back of the pod that had delivered Triana into—and back out of—the wormhole, it floated inside what appeared to be an old-fashioned aquarium. Gap's mother had kept exotic tropical fish in a similar container, and likely would have identified the contents as Gap had. But it was impossible . . . wasn't it?

Secured aboard a wheeled cart and covered with a sheet, it was moved to an isolated area in Sick House. Curious crew members along the way had stopped and followed the procession with their eyes, but nobody asked questions. Gap knew that it would dominate the conversation that evening in the Dining Hall and throughout the ship.

His next few hours had been spent alternating between Engineering—where the radiation shield was holding up, thanks to the energy siphon from the main engines—and the Spider bay. A thorough examination of the pod revealed no particular damage, other than an odd assortment of shorted-out electrical components. Other than the aquarium, there were no additional surprises.

Now the door to his room slid open and he stepped inside, mindful to be quiet. Daniil was sound asleep. Gap rarely had contact with his roommate these days; just another sign, he noted, that time off was overdue. His social life had withered away.

And, he realized, it was more insight into the life of Triana, or anyone with heavy responsibilities. It was the side of leaders rarely seen or understood.

Although his bed called out, he kicked off his shoes and checked his mail again. There was a single new entry, a note from Triana. Clicking on the file opened a group message to the Council, with a personal attachment for him. The main message called for the Council to assemble at seven in the morning—his shoulders sagged as he calculated the amount of sleep he would not be getting again this night—and thanked everyone for their great work during her absence. The note was short and to the point, in pure Triana style.

Standing behind his chair and leaning on the desk, he clicked open the attachment.

Gap, I'll certainly thank you in person, but didn't want to wait to let you know how grateful I am that you took charge of the ship while I was away. We haven't had a chance to talk yet, but I'm pretty sure you weren't happy about my decision to go. I know I put you in an awkward and difficult position, but I hope you understand that I had to do it.

We have a lot to cover, and some very important decisions to make. I'm glad to be back, and glad that you're on the team. And I'm glad you're such a good friend.

See you in the morning.

He couldn't think about any of that at the moment. If he didn't get some sleep he'd be worthless to Triana and the Council. Snapping off the vidscreen, he passed on his usual bedtime routine and simply fell onto his bed, covering his face with one arm, willing himself to clear his mind and find the shortest path to sleep.

It wasn't easy.

As always, Bon Hartsfield found escape in his work. Overseeing the Agricultural Department on the ship meant long hours anyway, but his office—tucked within one of the two massive domes atop *Galahad*—provided an insulated nest, especially this late at night.

The ship was programmed to simulate the natural day/night rhythms of Earth, which meant that the lights in many of the common areas slowly dimmed in the evening and then gradually grew brighter beginning around six in the morning. Now, while the majority of the Farms were lit only by the brilliant splash of stars through the clear domes, Bon's office was awash in light.

He stood behind his desk, inputting data from the latest harvest report. It was easily a task that could be entrusted to one of the workers under his supervision, but Bon preferred to remain busy. To sit idly—or worse, lie awake in bed—only invited the troubling thoughts to return. And there were far too many of those lately.

Topping them all was the startling return of Triana. Fight as he might to keep his mind elsewhere, the image of her slumped in the cockpit of the pod muscled its way back to the fore. Where had she been? What had happened to her on the other side of the wormhole? What was that . . . *thing* that she'd brought back?

Or had it brought *her* back?

And, most importantly, had his connection with the alien beings known as the Cassini created what Lita described as a beacon to guide Triana back to *Galahad*? How should he feel about that, when it was never his original intent?

The thoughts were overwhelming. He tossed his workpad stylus onto the desk and dropped into his chair. His blond hair, already long and unkempt, had grown shaggy from weeks of neglect and now fell across his face. At some point he'd need to either visit Jenner for a quick cut or chop it off himself.

It wasn't near the top of his priorities.

Triana's return, and his confused feelings regarding *Galahad*'s Council Leader; a raft of guilt over the death of Alexa, or rather, guilt over his inability to return her feelings; the news from Lita that his Cassini link had begun a physical transformation of his brain . . .

All of that in addition to a full workload in the Farms, and his stubborn reluctance to delegate as much as he should. Plus his Council duties.

A low guttural laugh escaped him. Council duties. He'd been almost invisible in Council meetings, speaking up only when irritation got the better of him, or when challenged by Gap. Those two events often went hand in hand. Yet he knew that his position as the head of the Agricultural Department came with leadership responsibilities, and he would never consider turning the Farms over to someone else. The soil, the crops—the very atmosphere of the domes—combined to create his personal haven aboard the ship.

The looming Council meeting would be exceptionally difficult. In a few hours Triana would begin the debriefing, and Bon dreaded the expected eye contact. He would, of course, sit sullenly and listen, but now—hours ahead of the meeting—he could already feel the burn of Triana's stare and the probing looks from Lita.

His head throbbed, a dull ache that was exacerbated, no doubt, by the seemingly nonstop activity of the past week combined with a lack of sleep. He had never requested a sleep aid of any sort, but now he wondered who might be manning Sick House at this late hour. Would they be required to report to Lita on every pill dispensed, or merely log the random request?

It wasn't worth the chance. Perhaps he could shut down his

brain through meditation. Just a few hours of sleep might cure the headache and give him the strength he needed to power through the morning meeting.

He killed the lights in his office, grabbed the blanket he kept stashed for nights like this, and stretched out on the floor.

Tor Teen Reader's Guide

About This Guide

The information, activities, and discussion questions that follow are intended to enhance your reading of *Cosmic Storm*. Please feel free to adapt these materials to suit your needs and interests.

Writing and Research Activities

I. Life in Space
   A. Many *Galahad* crew members keep mementos of their life and family from Earth. If you had been chosen to leave your family for a lifelong space expedition, what small keepsake might you choose to bring? Write a paragraph describing your keepsake, or create one using craft materials.
   B. Based on clues from the novel, draw a blueprint or sketch of *Galahad*, including the Spider bay, Sick House, Domes, cafeteria, and other areas mentioned in the story. Imagine

you are keeping a journal on behalf of the crew of *Galahad*. Write an entry describing your home in space to accompany your drawing.

C. Roc, the ship's computer, is an important character in *Galahad*. Make a list of at least ten ways that Roc assists the crew and/or ten quotes from the novel in which he gives advice to the humans aboard the ship. Then, with friends or classmates, debate whether or not *Galahad*'s designers' decision to give Roc a humorous personality was a good idea. Use your list to support your position.

D. Write a poem, short story, or song lyrics describing what it's like to live on a space ship traveling away from Earth, never to return.

II. Loss

A. Imagine you are a crew member aboard *Galahad*. Write several journal entries describing how you feel about the absence of Triana, the way the Council members are handling the need for a new leader, and the compromise to the ship's protective shield. What emotions—anger, fear, curiosity, nervousness, frustration, excitement—do you feel most?

B. With friends or classmates, role-play a conversation in which you give Bon, Lita, or Gap advice about dealing with their grief over the death of Alexa. If desired, use library or online resources to research ways to deal with grief and use this information in your role-play.

C. Did Triana make the right decision riding into the wormhole? In the character of Gap, Lita, Bon, or Channy, write an online journal entry confessing your true feelings about what happened when your leader went missing, and whether you think the crew of *Galahad* should allow her to resume her position upon her return.

III. Leadership

    A. What makes a great leader? Go to the library or online to learn more about great leaders through history. Choose one leader and create an informational poster about this individual. With friends or classmates, create a display of great leader posters.

    B. Make a class brainstorm list of important qualities for leadership. If possible, use information from activity III.A, above, to help you. When your list is complete, number the qualities in order of importance. Is there one quality which all leaders must share? Are there different but equally valid ways to lead? Write a short report analyzing your class list and discussion, and stating whether or not you agree with the conclusions of the class.

    C. Would your class vote for Gap or Hannah to become the new Council Leader? Hold an election in your classroom. Tabulate and report the results of the vote. Afterward, invite students to discuss how they chose their candidate.

    D. Learn more about politics in your city or town. Collect newspaper articles about upcoming elections. Write an article about local government for your school paper. Or volunteer to help with a political campaign. Write an essay explaining why it is (or, if you disagree, why it is not) important that young people participate in government.

    E. Who do you think won the *Galahad* election? What will happen next to the ship and its crew? Will the vultures attack? What do you think Triana brought back from the wormhole? Write one to three paragraphs describing your predictions for the next Galahad novel. Include a title suggestion if desired.

Questions for Discussion

1. The novel opens with Roc, the spaceship computer, commenting that, like wormholes, "rules change for people, too, depending upon what suits them at the time." Do you agree with this comment? To what kind of "rules" do you think Roc refers? As you read the novel, for which characters do you think the rules have changed? Which characters remain true to their beliefs and attitudes despite the current crisis?

2. Describe Gap's reaction to Triana's departure from the ship. How do Lita, Bon, and Channy seem to feel about the new leadership situation early in the novel? If you were a crew member on *Galahad,* would you be comfortable with Gap in charge?

3. Channy tells Bon there were "two people on this ship that you had feelings for, and they're both gone" (p. 24). Describe Bon's feelings for both of these people. How might Gap's feelings for Triana and Hannah put him in a similar emotional situation? Are either Gap or Bon able to discuss these feelings with others?

4. Why does Hannah decide to run for the position of Council Leader? Do you think her intentions are honorable? What qualities does she have that might make her a good choice for the position? What advice might you give her about her relationship with Merit?

5. Do you think Bon is right to refuse Gap's request to hold the translator until a new Council Leader is elected? Do you agree with Gap's decision to allow Bon to keep the translator until the election? Explain your answers.

6. How does Bon describe his relationship with the Cassini? Despite the pain, do you feel that he likes connecting with them? Can he resist them? If you were Bon, would you be worried about the Cassini's effects on your brain?

7. Compare the first and second election forums in terms of their structure, the attitudes of Gap and Hannah, and the reactions of the crowd. Do you think there was a clear winner or loser at either forum? Why or why not?

8. When Lita realizes that Bon was trying to reach Alexa and not Triana, how does this change her understanding of Bon? Do Bon's actions suggest that, despite his gruff exterior, he has some kind of faith? How might you describe that faith? How might this relate to the kind of faith Gap encourages the crew to find when he addresses them in the second election forum?

9. From "waves" to "bruises," what theory explaining the shield malfunctions is most convincing to you? Can you imagine living on a spaceship where your life was constantly, at some level, in peril? How do you think you might handle such stress? Does it make sense to you that members of the crew are acting out?

10. What is Lita's theory about Gap's connection with the Cassini and the events that have occurred since Triana left the ship? If Lita is correct, do you think Bon should be studied, restrained, or otherwise treated differently than the rest of the council and crew? If so, in what way and why?

11. How does the novel's final scene, in the Spider bay, reveal a change in the relationship between Gap and Bon? What other relationships have changed by the novel's end?

12. What has Gap learned about leadership and, perhaps, its relationship to friendship and even love by the novel's end? Has this novel affected the way you think about leadership roles you take on in your own life? Explain your answer.

© Photography De Sciose

DOM TESTA of Denver, Colorado, has been a radio show host since 1977 and currently is a cohost of the popular *Dom and Jane Show* on Mix 100 in Denver. Find out more about Dom at www.domtesta.com.

Can't wait for the next book in the series?

You're in luck . . .
join the Galahad community and
stay up-to-date on all things Galahad!

ClubGalahad.com is the official series website.
Go there __now__ to find:

- Exclusive updates from author Dom Testa
  - Access to special Galahad events
  - Cool, interactive stories and video
    - Triana's journal entries
      - And more!

Find it all at
ClubGalahad.com

and

Facebook.com/GalahadSeries

DON'T MISS A THING!